"Can you deny... respond to..."

"That's not the point," said Harriet desperately, and tried to pull away, but Leo laughed softly, and pulled her closer.

"If you prefer, we could just pretend to be engaged, just to give Nonna pleasure."

"Nonna would expect us to marry—you can't marry someone just to please your grandmother."

He bent his head and kissed her hungrily. "It would please *me*, also, believe me. And," he added, his voice deepening to a note that played havoc with Harriet's defenses, "I will take great pleasure in demonstrating how much it will please *you*."

CATHERINE GEORGE was born in Wales, and very early on developed a passion for reading, which eventually fueled her compulsion to write. Marriage to an engineer led to nine years in Brazil, but on his later travels the education of her son and daughter kept her in the U.K. And instead of constant reading to pass her lonely evenings she began to write the first of her romances. When not writing and reading she loves to cook, listen to opera, browse in antiques stores and walk the Labrador dog.

Catherine George makes a welcome return to Harlequin Presents®, with romance of the highest quality. Catherine loves to write about attractive characters, intriguing situations and emotionally intense relationships. Enjoy!

CHAPTER ONE

WHEN THE BORROWED SUITCASE came trundling into view Harriet felt a sudden, wild desire to snatch it from the carousel and fly straight back from Pisa to Heathrow. But as the bag drew near a male hand reached out for it and thwarted any rash idea of escape.

'Rosa,' said a deep, unmistakably Italian voice.

Harriet turned, resigned, to confront a man whose face had become as familiar as her own. But the photographs she'd pored over had failed to do him justice. Leonardo Fortinari, dressed in a casually elegant suit, was taller than expected. His eyes and hair were as dark as her own, and in the photographs taken several years back he'd been striking rather than handsome. But older, with the gloss and arrogance of maturity, he was formidable.

'Why, Leo, I'm honoured,' she returned, her smile deliberately mocking to cover her panic. 'I was about to catch a train. I didn't expect anyone to meet me.' Leo Fortinari least of all.

He shrugged negligently. 'I had business in Piza.' Ignoring the crowds jostling them, he stood still, looking her up and down with a frowning gaze so intent she felt it, tactile, on her skin. 'You have grown into a beautiful woman, Rosa.'

Harriet's heart thumped under her expensive borrowed jacket. 'Thank you,' she returned with determined composure. 'How is Nonna?'

'Delighted, naturally, by her prodigal's return. Come. I will drive you to the Villa Castiglione. She is impatient to see you.'

They were speeding along the autostrada before Leo Fortinari resorted to anything personal. 'I trust you have recovered, Rosa?'

Harriet shot a startled glance at him.

'From the tragedy of losing your parents,' he said gravely.

She bit her lip, taking refuge in silence.

His face softened slightly. 'I was sorry to miss the funeral.'

'Thank you for your letter,' she said. 'It was very kind.' And very stilted. As though he'd felt forced to write it.

The rest of the journey continued in far from comfortable silence. Leo Fortinari was courteous but distant, and by his manner obviously not of a mind to forgive the youthful Rosa. Good! In the present circumstances this disturbing man was best kept at a distance. It had never occurred to Harriet that she would have to face him so soon, that the great man himself would meet her at the airport. His younger brother Dante, possibly, or one of the Fortinari minions, never the great Leonardo himself. But on the plus side, it was a relief to get the encounter over with right away. Because as far as Harriet could tell she'd cleared one of the two most difficult hurdles. Now there was only Nonna, otherwise Signora Vittoria Fortinari, tonight. The meeting with the rest of the family, including Rosa's other cousins Dante and Mirella, was to be at the family party next day. If she survived that long. Harriet's tension mounted as the car bore her nearer and nearer the acid test of meeting Signora Fortinari. The journey led through undulating countryside dotted with ancient farms and grand country houses, with churches and bell towers here and there against a backdrop of vines and silver olive trees and dark, pointing figures of cypress. But Harriet had no eyes for it. As the car ate up the kilometres her sole thought was how to get through the weekend with no harm done to anyone. Herself included. She had always longed to return to Italy, it was true. But not desperately enough to embark on this present harebrained escapade. At least not until an offer had been made she was powerless, in the end, to refuse.

Harriet cast a look at her companion's forceful profile, relieved that Leo Fortinari had no inclination to talk to the passenger he believed was his cousin Rosa. Harriet sank lower in her seat as she thought of the moment at the Chesterton Hotel when Rosa Mostyn had sauntered into a private room full of women talking at the tops of their voices about the careers and husbands acquired since they'd left Roedale, the prestigious school for girls situated in beautiful Cotswold surroundings a few miles outside Pennington.

Harriet was an Old Roedalian herself. She'd won a scholarship at the age of ten, for one of the handful of day places in a school largely given over to boarders. A few days earlier the headmistress had rung Harriet to ask her to attend the reunion to praise the school's modern improvements to the contemporaries who had young daughters. And because Harriet was returning to Roedale to teach Modern Languages the following term she'd agreed. After a round of greetings and chitchat she'd been sipping a spritzer, won-

dering how soon she could get away, when Rosa
Mostyn appeared, the very last person Harriet had expected to see.

After eight years it was still a shock to come face-
to-face with someone who could have been her twin.
Rosa stood still in the doorway, her huge dark eyes
gazing round the sea of animated faces. Her hair hung
smooth, like black satin, to the shoulders of a suit cut
by some inspired, and probably Italian, designer, a
chunky gold ring on the hand she raised in salute as
she caught Harriet's eye. Sheer perfection, thought
Harriet, as she watched Rosa glide through the chat-
tering throng, greeting some people vivaciously, smiling politely at others she very obviously couldn't remember from Adam. She came to a stop at last beside
Harriet, smiling warily.

'Hello. Remember me?'

'How could I forget?' Harriet's answering smile
was wry when a ripple ran through the room as the
resemblance was spotted, remembered, and remarked
on. 'The waiter mistook me for you when I arrived.'

'Sorry about that.' Rosa hesitated. 'Are you with
anyone?'

Harriet shook her head. 'None of my set deigned
to turn up.'

'Mind if I tag along then?'

'Not in the least.'

Rosa gave her an expectedly grateful smile, then
tapped Harriet's left hand. 'No ring. Which doesn't
mean anything, of course. What do you do with yourself these days, Harriet?'

Wishing passionately she could say she was head
of a successful company, or some playboy billion-
aire's mistress, Harriet told Rosa the truth. 'I teach.

In fact I'm going back to Roedale to teach French and Italian next term. But at the moment I'm doing translations for a local firm which exports to Europe.'

Rosa nodded. 'You were always a whiz at languages.' She signalled to the barman. 'Vodka and tonic, please, and a refill for my friend.'

Harriet felt surprised. Rosa Mostyn and Harriet Foster had been anything but soul mates in the old days. Quite apart from the accidental resemblance, which both of them found deeply embarrassing, Harriet was a scholarship girl who travelled to school daily by bus, and worst of all, clever. Whereas Rosa was a boarder, more concerned with push-up bras than straight A's, and lived for the day when she could leave.

Harriet accepted the drink and raised it to Rosa in thanks. 'I didn't expect to see you here tonight.'

Rosa shrugged. 'I had no intention of coming. But I got a phone call at the last minute to say my date for the evening had fallen through. I was all dressed up with nowhere to go, so I thought, why not? My family owns the Chesterton Hotel and I could show my Mostyn nose to the staff here, and at the same time see how everyone's changed—or not,' she added, looking round the room.

'None of your cronies here, either,' commented Harriet. 'In school you could never move for them.'

Rosa smiled cynically. 'The Mostyn money, dear, not my charm and personality.'

They sipped in silence for a moment.

'I was sorry to hear about your parents,' said Harriet after a while.

'Thank you,' said Rosa quietly. 'They'd never flown on the same plane before the crash.' She downed her drink. 'Pity I'm driving, or I'd have another. How about your family? I remember your sister Kitty, tall, blonde and great at games—a lofty prefect when we were small fry.'

Harriet nodded. 'She's married now. My mother still lives in Pennington, but my father died when I was at University.'

'I'm sorry. I know how that feels.' Rosa eyed Harriet curiously. 'You're still single, then. No boyfriend?' She laughed suddenly. 'With your—or rather *our* looks—there must surely be men in your life?'

'None at the moment,' said Harriet lightly. 'How about you?'

Rosa's eyes lit up like lamps. 'I've actually met a man who couldn't care less about my money, for a change. After an early disaster I swore I'd leave the falling in love bit to the other sex. Then I met Pascal a few weeks ago and wham. Flat on my face. Can't eat, can't sleep. Hilarious, isn't it?'

'Does he feel the same way?'

Rosa sighed. 'I wish I knew. I met him when he was at the Hermitage covering a conference for a few days, but since then our encounters are few and far between. He's a foreign correspondent with a French newspaper.'

'Ah. Is that why the date fell through tonight?'

'Yes. He had to take off to cover some story half a world away, and couldn't make it. If not,' said Rosa with brutal honesty, 'I wouldn't be here in a roomful of squawking women. Present company excepted,' she added, grinning. 'You never squawked—too frighteningly composed, always.'

Harriet grimaced. 'Moody, you mean. I was a hugely difficult teenager. My family must have heaved a sigh of relief when I went away to college. After I qualified I got a teaching job in Birmingham. But my mother hasn't been well lately, so I've come back home for a while. And we're both enjoying the arrangement.' She glanced at her watch. 'Sorry, Rosa, but I promised the Head I'd do some networking— convince all the young marrieds that Roedale is *the* school for their daughters present and future.'

Rosa pulled a face. 'Rather you than me.' She hesitated for a moment. 'I don't suppose you'd fancy having supper with me somewhere afterwards?'

Taken aback for a moment, Harriet found she rather liked the idea. 'Why not? Give me half an hour.'

Which had been the beginning of it all. Harriet sighed heavily enough to attract a quizzical look from Leo Fortinari.

'Am I going too fast, Rosa? Are you nervous?'

Harriet smiled brightly. 'Yes. But not about your driving. I'm just wondering how Nonna will react to the sight of me.' Which was the truth as far as it went. Though sitting at close quarters with this self-assured Italian male was no help to relaxation, either. But Leo Fortinari would expect that. According to Rosa their parting years ago had been anything but cordial.

He turned his attention back to the road. 'You are different now, Rosa. At one time you had no nerves at all. But have no fear, Nonna forgave you long ago. We shall be with her in half an hour.'

Half an hour!

The supper with Rosa after the school reunion had been surprisingly enjoyable for Harriet. As schoolgirls they'd had nothing in common, but as adults they found a rapport totally unexpected to both of them.

After that first night they began going out together regularly, and when Rosa was even more blue than usual over Pascal's continued absence she would appear on the Foster doorstep, in need of sympathy both Harriet and her mother found easy to provide.

'Quite extraordinary,' said Claire Foster, the first time Harriet brought Rosa to the house. 'I saw you in school once or twice, of course. But the likeness is even more marked now you're older.'

'Only Harriet's smaller, and her hair curls,' said Rosa enviously, and coaxed Claire Foster to go out for a meal with them.

And when Claire protested she was too tired after a day of caring for her bedridden mother, Rosa, dressed to the nines, went off in her Alfa Romeo and bought fish and chips they ate straight from the packages at the kitchen table, the three of them giggling together like schoolgirls.

Before long all three of them were on close terms. Childhood friends had married and moved away, and Harriet's college friends were London based and she rarely saw any of them other than at a party or a wedding. Rosa filled a void Harriet hadn't even realised was there until the night of the reunion. And it was a relief to confess her worries to someone sympathetic. Claire Foster was on a hospital waiting list for a minor operation, and the rambling old family house was in desperate need of repairs Harriet's earnings as a translator couldn't begin to cover.

'Mother's forced to sell the house,' said Harriet one evening, over a meal in a wine bar.

'What a hassle for her, especially if she's not feeling well,' said Rosa, frowning. 'Does she mind?'

'Yes. Desperately. It's been the family home for

generations. She adores it.' Harriet leaned forward suddenly. 'Those men over there, staring at us. Do you know them?'

Rosa favoured the riveted males with a basilisk stare, then turned back to Harriet, winking. 'Just a couple of Romeos turned on by the resemblance.'

'I doubt it,' retorted Harriet. 'We're hardly a perfect match—me in my office gear, and you in those jeans. How you can breathe beats me, let alone sit down.'

'It's the cut, darling, they cost a fortune.' Rosa flushed suddenly. 'Sorry—tact was never my strong point.'

'Don't worry,' said Harriet, unperturbed.

Rosa looked at her steadily. 'Actually, Harriet, I do. I worry a lot.'

'About Pascal?'

'All the time,' admitted Rosa, sighing. 'But in this instance I mean Claire, and you. What happens to your grandmother if you get a smaller place?'

'She comes with us. At the moment she's got self-contained quarters upstairs, and we use the rest. But the idea of three of us cooped up together in some poky flat gives me nightmares!' Harriet shrugged, depressed. 'For some reason I've never been a favourite with Grandma. Kitty was her pet. But I've always felt unhappy—and guilty—because I find it so hard to love my grandmother, or even like her. Frankly, Rosa, she's a difficult lady. Which is nothing to do with age—she always was. And now she's bedridden and in pain quite a lot, poor dear, her fuse is even shorter.'

'I suppose she hates the thought of a nursing home?'

'Mother won't hear of it.'

'Your mother's a saint!' said Rosa emphatically.

'More than you know. Heaven knows how she had patience with me when I was a teenager.'

'I was no angel myself,' said Rosa soberly. 'But what was your problem?'

Harriet pulled a face. 'It makes me embarrassed to think of it now. I've never told anyone—not even Guy.'

'Who's Guy?' pounced Rosa.

'Ex-boyfriend.'

'Why ex?'

'He's Deputy Head at the school I taught at in Birmingham. When I left at the end of my first year to help Mother he objected, said I should put him first.'

'So exit Guy! Any regrets?'

Harriet shrugged. 'I missed him at first. Or maybe I just missed the social side and so on.'

'Was he good at the 'so on'?' asked Rosa, smiling wickedly.

Harriet grinned back. 'None of your business.'

'Which means he wasn't.'

'If anyone was lacking in that department it was me, Rosa.'

'No way,' said Rosa emphatically, her big eyes sparkling. 'Definitely Guy's fault if he couldn't ring your bell. Anyway, what were you going to tell me that you couldn't tell him?'

Harriet pulled a face. 'In my teens I got this bee in my bonnet, a fantasy about being adopted. I developed a real attitude—made my parents' life a misery.'

Harriet's youthful angst had been aggravated by her sister's teasing. Their father, Alan Foster, had been large and fair, like a throwback to some Viking invader—and Kitty was his image—while their tall, willowy mother had the chestnut hair and pale complexion of her own father.

'And then there was me,' said Harriet. 'Black hair and eyes, olive skin, and a head shorter than anyone else in the family. And at the mercy of teenage hormones. Kitty used to tease so much that I was a changeling, I began to believe it.'

'But you *weren't* adopted, surely!'

'No, of course I wasn't.' Harriet grinned sheepishly. 'Quite apart from the gruesome birth details Mother gave me when I was older, I've got a perfectly valid birth certificate confirming my pedigree. My looks are just some peculiar freak of genetics.'

Rosa was quiet for a moment. 'Talking of Kitty,' she said slowly, 'I know it's none of my business, but couldn't *she* help a bit, financially?'

'Not a chance. Kit's husband started up his own business recently, they've got a hefty bank loan, and she's pregnant, which means giving up her own job.' Harriet changed the subject swiftly. 'Anyway, enough of that. Tell me about Pascal. Still no news of him?'

Which was the question which had landed her where she was right now, thought Harriet despairingly, as her destination loomed nearer. Pascal Tavernier, it became plain as the weeks went by with no word, had left Rosa flat, without even the grace to tell her to her face.

'Since that last phone call, saying he was off to the Middle East, I haven't heard a word,' said Rosa unsteadily. 'And this morning, to cap it all, I got a letter from my grandmother, asking me to Tuscany for her eightieth birthday. I used to spend my summer holidays there at one time, but I haven't been back for years.'

'Why not?' asked Harriet curiously.

Rosa sighed. 'I was in my "rebel without a cause" stage, and Nonna's an autocrat of the first water. I behaved badly, did something she couldn't forgive. So I was expelled from Eden. Told to go home and stay there until I'd repented of my sins.'

'What did you *do,* for heaven's sake?'

Rosa was silent for a moment. 'I fibbed a bit,' she said at last, 'about Pascal being my first real love. At one time I had a terrific crush on my cousin, Leo. You know I'm half Welsh, half Italian. Leo's the Italian connection, a Fortinari, like my mother. He runs the family vineyards.'

'And?'

'I cringe to think of it, now, but I used to follow Leo round like a puppy. I was a much bigger nuisance than you ever were, Harriet, believe me.'

'But no response from Leo, I take it.'

'Not a flicker. So I decided to make him jealous by flirting with someone else. Leo was ten years older than me, and seriously unimpressed. Things got a bit out of hand at that point, so Nonna sent me home in disgrace.' Rosa shuddered involuntarily. 'When my parents died she was too ill with grief to come to the funeral, but she's been writing to me regularly since, and now, just when the timing's all wrong for me, she wants me in Fortino at last, to celebrate her birthday.' She sighed, and thrust a hand through her heavy hair. 'Harriet, I can't tell you how much I long to make my peace with Nonna. But I can't go.'

'Why not?'

'Not until I've heard from Pascal.' Rosa swallowed, suddenly deathly pale. 'Sorry—need a cloak-room.' She bolted, leaving Harriet staring after her in consternation.

Rosa was a long time in returning. When she slid into her seat at last her face was ashen and desperate, a look of such intense misery in her eyes Harriet put out a hand to cover hers.

'What's wrong?' she said gently. 'Is it Pascal?'

Rosa took in a deep, shaky breath. 'Serves me right, I suppose. Since Leo I've always called the tunes where men are concerned. But not this time. Pascal's obviously forgotten all about me.'

Harriet squeezed her hand. 'In which case, Rosa Mostyn, cross him off the list. Forget him.'

'Easier said than done,' said Rosa, with an unsteady smile. 'Pascal's left me something to remember him by.'

Harriet stared in dismay. 'You mean—?'

Rosa nodded desolately. 'I'm expecting Pascal's baby. I've tried to pretend it wasn't happening. But I can't ignore it anymore. And because I left the Villa Castiglione under a bit of a cloud, no way am I going back showing signs of being pregnant. If I had Pascal in tow as the prospective father, of course, it would be different. But not alone. Not like this,' she added hopelessly.

'Does your brother know?' asked Harriet, frowning.

'No way. Tony would go up like a rocket. In any case his wife Allegra's about to produce their first any minute, and she's not well. My little problem is the last thing either of them needs right now.'

Harriet's grasp tightened. 'Rosa, I'm so *sorry*. What can I do to help?'

Rosa's imploring black eyes locked with Harriet's. 'Will you go to Italy in my place? Pretend to be me for a weekend?'

'What?' Harriet pulled her hand away, staring at Rosa incredulously. 'You're joking!'

'You're the only one who could do it,' said Rosa rapidly. 'You look like me, you speak Italian fluently. And no one there has seen me for years, except at the funeral earlier this year. And that day my face was so blotched and swollen with crying I was unrecognizable anyway.' She leaned forward urgently. 'If you'll do this for me, Harriet, I'll pay for Claire's operation, get the repairs done on your house, *and* get someone in on a permanent daily basis to help with your grandmother.'

'Not on your life!' Harriet jumped up, her face rigid with offence. 'Some things you just can't buy, Rosa.'

Outside in the street Rosa caught Harriet by the arm. *'Please* don't be angry. I can't bear it.' She sighed heavily 'Look, for weeks I've been trying to find a way to help you and Claire, but I knew you wouldn't accept money from me. I hate to see your mother so unwell and exhausted. You, too, working by day, and helping with your grandmother at night. So look on this as a simple equation. You need money. I've got a lot of it. All I ask from you is two or three days spent at the Villa Castiglione as Rosa Mostyn. I'll provide the clothes and everything else you'll need. In return I'll ask my brother to send the Chesterton Hotel maintenance people over to your place, and I'll get your mother into hospital right away.'

Harriet, incensed, had refused point-blank. But later

on Rosa found an unexpected ally in Claire Foster. After listening to Rosa's sad little story, instead of supporting her daughter in her indignation, Claire reminded Harriet that it wasn't so long since she'd complained about the uneventfulness of life back in Pennington.

'Sounds like fun,' she said wistfully. 'In your place, darling, I'd do it like a shot. What an adventure!'

'And a profitable one for the Fosters, of course,' said Harriet tartly.

Claire winced, and Rosa rushed to put her arms around her, glaring at Harriet. 'How can you say such a hurtful thing to your mother? But even if it's true, why not? You're lucky you've still got a mother. You should jump at the chance to do this for her—' And to Harriet's dismay Rosa began to sob bitterly, burying her head on Claire's shoulder.

Harriet felt like a criminal as her mother comforted Rosa, and let her cry. But after a while Rosa sat up, scrubbed at her eyes, and apologized, sniffing hard.

'Sorry for the drama, folks. Hormones in a twist. Anyway it was a damn fool idea, Harriet. Forget it.' She turned to Claire. 'Look, you know I've become very fond of you both. So let me pay for the operation and the repairs anyway, Claire. *Please*. No strings. Except to let me come here now and then.'

'Wouldn't your brother object to a spot of moonlighting by his maintenance people?' said Harriet dryly.

Rosa scrubbed at her mascara stains. 'Not in the least, as long as I keep on making my Mostyn presence felt at both hotels while his attention's on Allegra. Tony owes me.'

On her return home in disgrace from Italy Rosa's

penance had been a job at the Hermitage, the lavish Mostyn hotel in the country. Outraged by his mother-in-law's letter, which caused a rift never to be healed, Huw Mostyn put Rosa to work as kitchen help at first, and from there she worked her way upwards through various jobs until her father finally sent her on a management course she took to like a duck to water.

'Rosa,' said Claire gently, 'why has it taken so long for your grandmother to want you back?'

'Because I flatly refused to repent and apologize,' said Rosa, biting her lip. 'Besides, after being packed off home like that I just couldn't face going back again. I did repent in time, but by then it was far too late to apologize, stubborn fool that I am.'

Harriet jumped up as her grandmother's bell rang. 'You stay there, Mother.'

Enid Morris, as usual, wanted Claire, but Harriet explained that her mother was tired, saw to her grandmother's most intimate needs, settled her back in bed with her book and her spectacles, doled out her pills, placed a drink in exactly the right place, found the right channel on the television, then rearranged the pillows several times until the invalid was grudgingly satisfied. Harriet went downstairs afterwards deep in thought. Her mother, in poor health herself, performed these same tasks dozens of times a day, and not only coped with a querulous invalid, but with the laundry, shopping, and cooking that went with the job. Harriet felt sudden shame. All that was needed, to make life a little easier all round, was a trip to the Italy she adored, pretending to be Rosa Mostyn for a couple of days. As only Harriet Foster was equipped to do.

Harriet paused at the foot of the stairs, looking into

the hall mirror. She stared hard and long at her reflection, which, she couldn't deny, was a mirror image of Rosa's. She lingered outside the sitting room door, listening to Rosa talking to Claire, and even to her own hypercritical ear, she could have been listening to herself. Both of them had husky voices, with a distinctive little catch that Guy Warren, in a fit of frustrated rage, had once termed misleading because it was so sexy.

Harriet waited a minute longer, then thrust open the door, and before she could change her mind, said, 'All right, Rosa, I'll do it. I'm probably mad, and I'm sure to regret it, but as Mother said, it's an adventure. As long as your grandmother isn't harmed in any way by the switch, I'll pretend to be her loving granddaughter for a day or two. But this is a one-off, Rosa. Afterward you'll just have to tell her about the baby.'

CHAPTER TWO

HARRIET'S TENSION INCREASED as the purring Maserati turned off on a narrow road which wound up a hill in dizzying curves. Leonardo Fortinari drove his petrified passenger through an entrance flanked by stone pillars into the steep, tiered gardens of the Villa Castiglione, and stopped at the foot of well-worn steps leading to a balustraded terrace adorned with small, time-worn statues and stone urns spilling flowers. After a glance at her taut face he touched a hand fleetingly to her denim-clad knee.

'Courage, Rosa.'

To her secret consternation his touch seared through the denim like a brand. Harriet sat very still to disguise her reaction, her eyes fixed on the two-story building. The house was as familiar from a photograph as Leo Fortinari, but unlike the man beside her it was smaller than expected, old and very beautiful, built of venerable gold stone, with an arcaded loggia on three sides.

'Before we go in,' said Leo curtly, 'do nothing this time, Rosa, to upset Nonna in any way. She is valiant, as always, but she has not been in good health lately. She was insistent you came back to see her again because she believes her time is short. Do nothing to shorten it. Understood?'

Annoyed by his dictatorial tone Harriet gave him a disdainful look. 'Nothing's changed, then. You still believe the worst of me.' This was Rosa's firm belief, and so far Leo Fortinari was doing nothing to contradict it.

He gave a short, mirthless laugh. 'Do you blame me?'

Harriet said nothing. If in doubt, say nothing and look mysterious, had been Rosa's instructions. Sensible ones, probably. If anything about this entire situation could be described as remotely sensible. Harriet got out of the car before Leo could touch her again in assistance, slung the strap of Rosa's expensive leather bag over her shoulder and followed him inside.

A small, beaming woman came bustling towards them across the cool, marble-floored hall, greeting Leo in a flood of whispered Italian in a strong local accent Harriet had to concentrate hard to understand.

'Welcome, Miss Rosa,' she added in an undertone. 'You must be tired. I shall bring coffee before I take you to your room. The signora is sleeping. You will see her later.'

'You remember Silvia, of course,' said Leo, as the woman went off.

'No. She's new since I was last here.'

And thank heaven for that, thought Harriet, as he ushered her into a room Rosa had described in such painstaking detail that the abundance of pictures, gilt-framed mirrors and carved furniture was reassuringly familiar. Making no attempt to hide her nerves, she sat down on a sofa upholstered in faded ruby velvet, desperate to get the meeting with the signora over with. Though if Leo hadn't spotted the switch, she comforted herself, perhaps no one else would, either. Like Rosa, she had no telltale distinguishing marks. And to make Harriet word-perfect in her role, Rosa had brought dozens of photographs and letters to the Foster house, recounting every detail of her family she could think of as Harriet took reams of notes which she read over and over in bed every night until she knew them by heart.

'How quiet you are,' said Leo, giving her a leisurely scrutiny as he pulled up a chair. 'You have changed with maturity, Rosa. You are thinner, also your hair curls.'

'Clever hairdresser,' she said, unruffled, prepared for this. 'Do you approve?'

Leo's jaw tightened. 'You know very well that you are beautiful, Rosa.'

Harriet's eyes fell before his cold, assessing gaze, then she looked up with a smile, thanking Silvia as the woman came in to set down a large tray with coffee and tiny sweet biscuits, before rushing off to rejoin the women preparing tomorrow's feast in the kitchen.

'I had forgotten that faint, charming accent, Rosa,' he said, watching her as she poured.

Rosa had told Harriet Leo liked his coffee black, but she looked him in the eye and offered him cream. 'Since I was banished I haven't needed Italian much. Though it comes in useful in my job.' Which was entirely true.

'So you have forgotten I like my coffee black and sweet,' commented Leo. A black eyebrow arched. 'What else have you forgotten, Rosa?'

'As much as I possibly could,' she said tartly. 'Will you have a biscuit?'

Leo shook his head, and leaned back, watching her through the steam from his cup. 'So. How do you like working at the Hermitage?'

'More than I expected to when I started,' said Harriet, quoting Rosa.

His eyes held hers relentlessly. 'You had different ambitions once.'

'Modelling, you mean.' Harriet shrugged. 'Just teenage daydreams. I've recovered from those. Every last one of them,' she added deliberately.

'Have you, indeed?' The black-lashed eyes narrowed. 'You were beautiful enough for modelling. Even more so now time has wrought certain changes,' he added, eyeing her up and down with a look which seemed to register everything from the exact shade of her lipstick to the size of her shoes.

Harriet turned away to refill her coffee cup, wishing Leo Fortinari would remove his disturbing presence and take himself off to his famous vineyards, which she had learned were several kilometres away from the Villa Castiglione.

'How are Mirella and Dante?' she asked politely.

'Dante is my right hand since my father's retirement. Mirella, as you know, is married now. She is already expecting her first child.' Leo leaned forward to replace his cup on the tray. 'So is Tony's wife, I hear.'

Harriet nodded. 'Any moment now, which is why they couldn't come for Nonna's birthday.'

'I hope everything goes well for her. Mirella, thankfully, is in the best of health.' His eyes narrowed to a taunting gleam. 'You did not come to her wedding.'

He was baiting her, thought Harriet angrily. 'For obvious reasons,' she retorted, staring him down.

'You mean you were afraid to come?'

She shrugged. 'If you like.'

'Would you have come if Nonna had invited you personally before this?' he asked, leaning nearer. 'Or were you afraid of meeting old friends?'

'Stop bullying the child,' said a voice from the doorway.

Leo rose to his feet, and Harriet followed suit quickly, her heart in her throat. The woman advancing towards her was dressed in a dark blue linen suit of exquisite cut. Her once dark hair was streaked with white, but faultlessly arranged, her face skilfully made up and she wore her years with grace and panache. Harriet gazed at her mutely, fighting to control her panic, then Vittoria Fortinari held out her arms, her huge eyes glittering with tears, and Harriet moved guiltily into her embrace.

'Rosa,' said the other woman unsteadily, holding Harriet at arms' length. 'How beautiful you are—' She broke off to dab a handkerchief to her eyes. 'But I must not cry. The make-up will melt.' She smiled, looking so mischievous Harriet smiled back involuntarily.

Signora Fortinari drew Harriet down to sit beside her on the sofa, then smiled up at Leo, who was watching them with the intent, probing look Harriet was rapidly growing to dislike. 'Thank you for bringing Rosa to me, Leo.'

In response to such sweet, but definite dismissal Leo Fortinari bowed formally. 'I see I have served my purpose, Nonna, so I shall go back to Fortino.'

'Now I have offended you,' observed his grandmother placidly. 'Come back to dinner later, Leo,' she added, to Harriet's dismay.

Leo, noting it, smiled sardonically. 'If Rosa does not object, of course.'

'I'd be delighted,' Harriet lied.

'Good,' said Vittoria, smiling benignly. 'Bring Dante with you, Leo. He will be eager to see Rosa again.'

Harriet relaxed a little. Dante had been in California when Rosa had blotted her youthful copybook.

'Whatever you wish, Nonna,' said Leo, and raised his grandmother's hand to his lips with practiced grace. 'But I think you should be resting tonight, in preparation for tomorrow's celebrations.'

'But then, you are not *always* right, Leonardo,' she said gently.

Leo Fortinari acknowledged the hit with a raised hand, said his goodbyes in a way which encompassed Harriet without actually addressing her individually, and departed with the faintest hint of swagger in his retreat.

'Now,' said Signora Fortinari with satisfaction. 'Tell me everything about yourself, my child—'

'First, please let me make my apologies,' said Harriet swiftly, following Rosa's instructions. She took a deep breath. 'Nonna, I know this is long overdue, but I'm desperately sorry for what happened.'

'And I should have been more understanding—and forgiving,' said Vittoria sombrely, and took Harriet's hand. 'Let us talk of it no more. You are here now, and that is all that matters. Pride is a terrible thing, Rosa, and I am guilty of it. I should have mended the rift with your father, and not allowed Leo to influence me so much. He was always so adamant that seeing you again would reopen old wounds and endanger my health. But he was wrong. Life is too short for such foolishness.'

Harriet nodded soberly, thinking of Rosa's parents.

'Who should know better than you, child?' For a moment Vittoria Fortinari looked every moment of her age, and more, then she straightened and summoned a smile. 'Now tell me, Rosa, have you brought a beautiful dress to wear tomorrow night?'

Harriet confessed to bringing more than one. Rosa had provided her with two stunning creations with mouth-watering labels, each of them worn only once.

After bringing the signora up to date on Rosa Mostyn's current life and job, taking care to omit any reference to Pascal Tavernier in the process, Harriet reported on the precarious health of Allegra Mostyn.

'Tony is driving everyone mad, Allegra included, because he's in such a state,' said Harriet.

'It is a fortunate that men are not obliged to give birth,' said Vittoria dryly. 'Otherwise the human race would have died out long ago.'

Harriet's appreciative chuckle turned into a yawn, and the other woman patted her hand affectionately.

'Silvia has taken up your luggage. Go up to your room and have a bath and a rest before dinner, my child. You look tired. I shall visit the kitchen, and interfere with all the preparations for tomorrow. Because of them dinner tonight will be just a simple cold meal.'

'I'll enjoy that,' Harriet assured her, and accompanied the signora across the square hall. The shallow, worn stone stairs led up to a gallery which ran round three sides of the renaissance-style colonnade of arches in the hall below.

'You are in your old room, cara,' said Vittoria, and kissed Harriet's cheek. 'Sleep, if you can. We shall eat at eight.'

Very much aware that the signora was watching

with a fond smile, Harriet went upstairs slowly, praying she could find the right room. Following the di-
agram etched in her brain Harriet turned left at the
head of the stairs, counted three doors along on the
right, and sure enough, an open door revealed Rosa's
luggage standing at the foot of a carved wood bed in
a room where everything, down to the last ornament,
was just as Rosa had described it. Harriet closed the
door behind her and leaned against it, letting out a
sigh of heartfelt relief. So far so good. Two hurdles
cleared. Only Dante and Mirella left. But Rosa had
been certain there would be no trouble with Leo's
younger brother and sister. The most dangerous fly in
the ointment, she'd warned, was Leo himself. Harriet
cursed herself for failing to hide her dismay when his
grandmother commanded him to dine with them. Leo
had been amused by it, damn the man. Now that
Signora Fortinari had accepted her without hesitation
it was obvious that Rosa was right. Leo was the main
danger.

Rosa had strongly advised against being friendly
with Leo Fortinari. Harriet was to be as cool and distant as she liked, because that was how Rosa would
have behaved if she'd come herself. If only she had!
thought Harriet wearily, and blessed the industrious
Silvia when she found her clohes unpacked and put
away. Feeling more criminal than ever she shut herself into the bathroom and used Rosa's cellphone to
call her mother, and after a swift report on initial success, promised to ring next day and asked Claire to
pass on the news.

Later, after a bath and a rest among the cool linen
sheets of the bed, Harriet felt a lot better. Wrapped
in a dressing gown she stood at the window for a

while, able to enjoy the view to the full now there was no hostile male presence to spoil it for her. She had spent time in Siena during her language course, and had fallen in love with Italy the moment she arrived. The view from the Villa Castiglione rekindled the passion as she gazed at violet-shadowed hills rolling away into the fading light. The village in the foreground was far enough below to be a mere jumble of umber walls and cinnamon roofs clustering round a church and a slender tower where a bell began to peal as she watched. Harriet listened with delight, and relaxed at last as she breathed in the remembered scent of Tuscany.

When starlit darkness eventually hid the view Harriet turned back into the room and switched on lamps, then threw open the doors of the carved armoire and eyed the selection of clothes Rosa had provided. The borrowed jeans she'd worn with a lightweight jacket for travelling were the kind of thing she wore herself, though with less famous labels. But for more formal wear Rosa had a liking for clothes totally foreign to anything Harriet owned. Once her hair was dry she smoothed on a dress knitted from cobweb-fine topaz wool, with a long skirt which curved over the hips and clung at the knees in a way which suggested a mermaid's tail. Thankful for an inch less than Rosa above and below the waist Harriet added the matching jacket to mitigate the second-skin effect a little, then made up her face with Rosa's cosmetics, emphasizing her eyes as patiently instructed. She slid her feet into bronze pumps with tall, slender heels, then gave her reflection a mocking salute with a hand embellished with Rosa's heavy, pearl-studded gold ring.

When Harriet went downstairs she took a peep into a dining room laid ready for dinner, then crossed the hall to find Rosa's grandmother enthroned on the ruby velvet sofa, with a tray of drinks beside her.

'Rosa, how elegant!' she exclaimed.

Harriet bent to kiss the cheek held up for the caress. 'So are you, Nonna.'

'Come, pour yourself a glass of wine, and sit beside me while we wait. Tell me about Tony and his new wife. Do you like her?'

Harriet told everything she'd learned about the unknown Tony and Allegra, and their excitement over their first baby, then broke off to nibble hungrily on a bread stick wound with prosciutto. But she chose sparkling water to drink. Having come this far without mishap it seemed best to avoid the tongue-loosening properties of Fortinari wine.

'You are hungry, child. You should have asked Silvia for something to eat,' scolded Vittoria.

'I just wanted coffee when I arrived,' said Harriet, taking another bread stick. 'And I can never eat on the plane. I hate flying.'

'Do you, dearest?' Vittoria Fortinari looked surprised. 'You used to love it when you were a child.'

Oops, thought Harriet. Careful. 'I'm not so keen these days—' she halted abruptly as the other woman's eyes filled with sudden tears.

'Of course you are not, Rosa,' said Vittoria huskily, and dabbed a handkerchief to her eyes. 'Forgive me.'

Harriet's arms went out involuntarily, and Vittoria clasped her close. They stayed immobile for several seconds, both of them deeply contrite, for different reasons, for bringing up the subject of flying.

'Good evening.'

Harriet drew away swiftly from the scented, comforting embrace of Rosa's grandmother to see Leonardo Fortinari approaching across the faded, beautiful carpet. Less formal, but equally impressive in an open-necked shirt under a linen jacket a shade or two paler than his perfectly cut fawn trousers, he gave Harriet a slow, all-encompassing look which travelled up to her eyes at last and stayed there.

'I agree that Rosa looks beautiful this evening, but stop staring at her,' said his grandmother severely. 'You are late—and where is Dante?'

Leo removed his gaze with visible effort, and turned to his grandmother. 'Forgive me, Nonna. Dante makes his apologies,' he said, stooping to kiss her. 'He is detained in Arezzo, and will not be home until late. But he promised to be first here tomorrow night.' He turned to Harriet. 'Your rest has transformed you, Rosa.'

'Thank you,' she returned with composure.

'But she is hungry,' said Vittoria, and rang a small silver bell. 'Let us go straight to the table.'

Harriet made appreciative murmurs as she was served with pasta in savoury meat sauce for the first course of the meal Vittoria Fortinari had warned would be simple, due to the industry still raging in the kitchen as they dined.

'It was always your favourite,' she said affectionately, as Harriet made short work of her pasta.

'With such appetite it is a wonder you stay so slender,' observed Leo, watching her. 'You were much rounder once.'

'I work hard,' said Harriet. So did Rosa, despite her money.

'Is Tony so relentless in keeping you tied to the

Hermitage?' queried Leo, leaning nearer to fill her water glass.

Aware that Vittoria Fortinari was awaiting her answer with deep interest Harriet met his black-lashed eyes serenely. 'Not at all. I answer to no one but myself. Now. When my parents died I inherited a substantial sum of money, as I'm sure you know. I work in the family business because I want to, not because I'm forced to. And at the moment, while Tony is so anxious about Allegra, I divide myself between the Hermitage out in the country, and the Chesterton in Pennington, to give him more time with her.'

Signora Fortinari nodded approvingly. 'In his letter Tony told me he is very grateful for this.'

Leo Fortinari shook his head in mocking admiration. 'It is hard to believe that reckless little Rosa has changed into such a responsible adult.'

His grandmother eyed him coldly. 'It is time, Leonardo, that we put the past behind us, and enjoy the present. What little I have left of it,' she added, laying a dramatic hand on her heart.

'Nonna, you will live to be a hundred,' he assured her, but from then on his manner became noticeably less hostile to the prodigal granddaughter.

Rosa's teenage episode obviously rankles with him even now, thought Harriet, as the plates were removed. Leo, apparently taking his grandmother's words to heart, helped both women to thin slices of spiced ham, and to the accompanying salad of cheese and ripe red tomato slices dressed with olive oil and basil. Harriet accepted his attentions politely, but listened with genuine interest as he talked of the latest Fortinari Chianti Classico.

'Is that what we're drinking?' asked Harriet.

Leo raised his eyebrows. 'No, little savage. This is from the 1997 vintage—the best for fifty years. Nonna has opened it in honour of your return.'

'Instead of the fatted calf?' said Harriet, smiling, and willed Leo to change the subject. One of the many differences between herself and Rosa Mostyn, was her very un-Italian ignorance of wine.

'A fondness for wine was never one of your failings, darling,' said Vittoria, startling Harriet by her insight. 'At least,' she added, eyes twinkling, 'not when you were seventeen.'

Nor was it for Harriet now she was nine years older than that. Wine was an unaffordable luxury in the Foster household.

'So, Rosa,' said Leo, leaning back in his chair, 'you are an important aid to the running of the Mostyn empire.'

Harriet was getting tired, and finding it hard to concentrate. She spoke Italian fluently enough, but an entire evening of conversation in a foreign tongue, while simultaneously trying to maintain a faultless impersonation of Rosa, was beginning to tell. 'Two hotels can hardly be called an empire,' she pointed out.

'True,' he allowed. 'But they are successful, and well known to foreign visitors for their luxury and comfort. Perhaps I shall come and stay at your Hermitage, and sample the Mostyn hospitality myself one day.'

'By all means,' said Harriet, secure in the knowledge that if he did the real Rosa Mostyn would have the pleasure of entertaining him. A thought which gave her a sudden, unaccountable pang she put down to indigestion.

Signora Fortinari instructed Silvia to serve coffee in the salon. 'Rosa has brought something beautiful to wear to my party,' she informed Leo, as he helped her up from the table.

'She could scarcely look more ravishing than she does tonight,' he said, giving Harriet a smouldering look which clenched secret muscles in response under the clinging gossamer wool.

'True,' agreed his grandmother, 'but tomorrow is a special occasion.'

Harriet detached her gaze from Leo's with effort. 'And because of it, I've actually brought two dresses. Tomorrow Nonna can choose which one she prefers.'

After the meal they went back to the salon to drink coffee under the painted cherubs on the exquisite, faded ceiling.

'You always liked the putti,' said Leo casually, following Harriet's eyes. 'You were fond of one in particular.'

'The trumpeter blowing in his friend's ear,' agreed Harriet, blessing Rosa's memory for detail.

'You look tired, dearest,' said Signora Fortinari lovingly. 'Drink your coffee, then off you go to bed so that you will be fresh and sparkling for my celebration tomorrow.'

'Signora?' said Silvia from the door. 'Could you come, please?'

'Another crisis,' said her mistress with a sigh as Leo helped her to her feet.

'I will keep Rosa entertained until you return,' he assured her.

Harriet received the news with mixed feelings, hoping the problem in the kitchen would be resolved quickly, before Rosa's formidable cousin tripped her up in some way.

'Perhaps you would care to go out onto the loggia?' he suggested. 'Even the moon is obedient to Nonna's wishes for a perfect birthday.'

Welcoming the idea of concealing moonlight Harriet went out ahead of him and leaned her hands on the balustrade as she gazed at the panorama before her. The summits of the rolling hills were bathed in bright moonlight, but a thin veil of mist added an ethereal touch to the half-hidden village below.

'I'd forgotten how beautiful it is,' she said quietly. Which was true. Each time she'd returned to Northern Italy in her student days her reaction had been the same.

'And I had forgotten how beautiful *you* are, Rosa,' said Leo softly, his eyes on her profile. 'You have changed so much it is hard to believe you once caused me—and not only me—so much trouble.'

'I was very young, Leo. I'm not the same person I was then.' Her mouth twisted wryly at the truth of it. 'Surely it's a good thing that I've changed?'

'Very good,' he said huskily, and moved closer. 'So good that perhaps now is the time to kiss and be friends.'

CHAPTER THREE

ROSA HAD BEEN RATHER VAGUE about the exact nature of the trouble with Leo Fortinari, but since it seemed likely kissing had come into it somewhere Harriet stepped back, determined to avoid stirring up any extra trouble on Rosa's behalf. Or her own.

'You disagree?' said Leo. His voice dropped half an octave, causing turbulence Harriet's clinging dress failed to disguise from him. His eyes dropped to the hurried movement of her breasts, and she turned away quickly, her hot hands grateful for the cold stone of the balustrade.

'No games, please, Leo,' she said acidly. 'I'm not seventeen anymore.'

'No, you are not,' he whispered, moving close behind her.

Harriet tried hard to control her breathing as she felt the heat of his body penetrate through her dress. She tensed, feeling his breath on her neck as his hands appeared either side of hers on the balustrade, preventing her escape.

'As Nonna said,' he breathed against her hair, 'it is time to forget—and forgive—the past. The present is so much more appealing, Rosa.' She tensed as his arms slid round her from behind, his hands cupping her breasts, his mouth pressed to the hollow behind her ear.

Harriet stood motionless, head bowed, her hands clenched on the balustrade as she controlled her mutinous senses, forcing them to ignore the fire his caressing hands and lips sent streaking through her body. Stay cool and distant, she told herself wildly, and by superhuman effort controlled every muscle and quivering nerve in her body, as she battled with the urge to twist round in Leo Fortinari's arms and surrender her mouth to the lips now moving along her jaw.

It seemed an eternity before Leo became convinced of the message she was sending him, but at last he moved away, breathing audibly, and leaned, arms folded, against one of the columns of the loggia. From the corner of her eye Harriet saw him staring down at the view below, his profile hard and cold as marble in the moonlight.

'When you were young you desired my caresses, Rosa,' he said harshly.

Harriet wanted them right now, a discovery which rendered her speechless.

'You were a most persistent charmer in those days,' he went on, as though they were discussing the weather. 'You threatened to kill yourself if I spurned your rash little overtures.'

'Emotional blackmail,' said Harriet wearily. 'Teenage hormones on the rampage. As you can see, I didn't carry out my threat.'

'For which,' he said smoothly, turning a dark, discerning eye on her, 'we are all grateful, Rosa.'

'Are you?'

Leo smiled, his teeth showing white in the half light. 'If you tried your wiles on me now, I would be more receptive.'

Harriet suppressed a shiver at the thought of it.

'You are cold?' he said instantly. 'Let me give you my jacket—'

'No,' she said quickly, and turned towards the open doorway. 'Let's go inside.'

Indoors, in the warm light from the lamps in the salon, Harriet was composed enough to smile politely into Leo's watchful face as she resumed her place on the sofa.

'Will I know all the guests at the party tomorrow?' she asked, determinedly conversational. Rosa had made a list of likely people, and described their background and relationships, but if Leo had any helpful information Harriet was keen to add it to her research.

'Mainly the family and a few of Nonna's friends. Why? Will that bore you?' he asked cuttingly.

Harriet shook her head, determined, if it killed her, to keep things pleasant. 'No. But it's years since I was here. I'm worried I won't remember everybody.'

Leo gave her a smile which raised the hairs along her spine. 'In that case, little cousin, I shall stay very close at all times to whisper reminders in your ear.'

'Bravo,' approved Signora Fortinari, coming to join them. 'It is good to see you together, friends again.'

'For you, Nonna, anything that makes you happy,' declared Leo. 'But now I must leave. I have many things to do before I seek my lonely bed.'

His grandmother reached up to kiss his cheek. 'Try to seek it a little earlier tonight, my love.'

He laughed affectionately, and patted her hand. 'Have no fear, Nonna. I shall make sure that Dante, Mirella and Franco all arrive in good time tomorrow.'

'Such a pity that your mother and father are in California,' sighed the signora. 'But I absolutely forbade them to cut short their holiday.' A sudden smile lit the magnificent dark eyes. 'And to make up for their absence I have Rosa.'

'For which, of course, we all rejoice,' said Leo smoothly, and moved to stand over Harriet. 'Good night, cousin. I shall see you tomorrow.'

She tensed, afraid for a split second that he intended to kiss her. Instead he raised her hand to his lips, looking into her eyes to gauge her reaction as he deliberately touched his tongue to her hot skin.

She pulled her hand away and bade him a very husky good night, her colour heightened. With a look of triumph in his eyes he bowed gracefully, turned away to embrace his grandmother, then left them alone together.

Vittoria Fortinari turned to Harriet with a happy sigh. 'Now, darling, what would you like to drink before we go to bed?'

Harriet had trouble in getting to sleep that night, her wakefulness nothing to do with the fear of discovery, or the strange bed, or even nerves about the party. The problem was Leo Fortinari. For some reason she'd taken it for granted she would feel as hostile towards him as Rosa did. It had never occurred to her that she would be so powerfully attracted to him. On the moonlit loggia it had taken every last scrap of will-power she possessed to withstand the persuasion of his mouth and skilled, arousing fingertips. Harriet shivered, her face burning as she felt her nipples rise and harden against the silk of Rosa's nightgown. If he'd kissed her mouth... She flipped over in the bed, her hands clenched in the pillow as she burrowed her face into it.

What was Leonardo Fortinari up to? she thought

stormily. According to Rosa he had been the deciding factor in her exile from Fortino all these years. And right up to the little interlude on the loggia his attitude had shown small sign of change. Which had made his lovemaking all the more shocking. Harriet gritted her teeth. Her main worry now was nothing to do with the guests at the party, only the fact that Leo had promised—or threatened—to stay close by her side all night to supply the missing names. A prospect which did nothing at all for her insomnia.

Vittoria Fortinari's birthday dawned bright and sunny, chilly enough at the Villa's altitude for Harriet to put on one of Rosa's sweaters over her shirt and jeans to eat breakfast. She stole downstairs, holding a large shiny carrier bag behind her back, and met Silvia in the hall, carrying a large tray into the salon.

'Good morning. The signora will be with you in a moment,' gasped the plump little woman, as she put the tray down on a table. 'She ordered breakfast in here just for today. The dining room is ready for the party.'

'Can I do anything to help?' asked Harriet, hiding the bag behind a chair.

Silvia looked doubtful. 'But the signora—'

'I'd like to help,' said Harriet firmly.

'In what way, exactly?' asked Vittoria Fortinari, hurrying into the room. 'Good morning, darling. You can bring the coffee in now, Silvia, please.'

'Good morning, and happy, happy birthday,' said Harriet, kissing Rosa's grandmother with an affection she found remarkably easy. Her own grandmother would have pushed her away irritably if she'd tried anything so demonstrative.

'Thank you, Rosa.' Vittoria beamed, looking so

happy Harriet banished all her qualms about the impersonation and set herself to make the day as special for Rosa's grandmother as possible.

They sat down with plates on their knees in picnic fashion, the older woman obviously enjoying the novelty as they ate slices of melon and ate hot rolls fresh from the bakery in the village before finishing all the coffee Silvia brought them. While they ate Harriet volunteered her skill at table-laying, and at folding napkins into flower shapes, skills Vittoria took to be part of Rosa's training at the Hermitage, but which had actually been acquired in less exalted catering establishments during Harriet's university vacations.

'I really would like to help,' said Harriet, meaning it on her own behalf, and at the same time hoping the offer would win points for Rosa.

'Then you shall,' said the signora fondly. 'I can set a table well enough, but transforming napkins into flowers is beyond me, alas. And certainly beyond Silvia and the helpers we've brought in from the village.'

Once Silvia had cleared away, Harriet reached behind her chair for the large scarlet bag and handed it over. 'Happy birthday again, Nonna.'

Signora Fortinari received the bag with girlish excitement, exclaiming at the number of parcels inside. Knowing that Rosa had taken endless time and care to think of a gift that would please her grandmother most, Harriet watched, feeling tense on Rosa's behalf, as Vittoria unwrapped a box and lifted the lid, then stared down at its contents with eyes which filled with tears she dashed instantly away. She took out the photograph with unsteady hands, one finger smoothing the chased silver frame as she gazed down at the faces of her daughter and son-in-law, taken only a month before the air crash.

Rosa had taken the photograph herself on her parents' last anniversary. Happy and smiling on a sunlit afternoon on the beach where the family had gathered for a picnic, the couple were laughing at the camera, their arms around each other.

For a moment, as she watched, Harriet experienced a painful sense of intrusion. Then she forced herself back into the role she was playing, and cleared her throat. 'I thought you'd like to remember them like that. I hope it hasn't made you sad.'

Rosa's grandmother put the photograph down very gently, then embraced Harriet, kissing her tenderly. 'Such a beautiful thought, Rosa. Thank you, my darling.'

'Open the rest, then,' commanded Harriet huskily. 'Another one from me, and one each from Tony and Allegra.'

Rosa's second gift was a cashmere sweater and long cardigan in a subtle shade of rose pink, and Signora Fortinari promptly tried on the cardigan, and pronounced it perfect. She kept it on as she unwrapped Tony's present, which was a set of photograph frames, but in gold leaf and empty this time, ready to frame studies of the new little Mostyn when he arrived.

'They know it is a son?' said the prospective great-grandmother in wonder.

'Modern technology, Nonna,' said Harriet.

Allegra's present was a whole range of wickedly expensive skin-care products, which Tony, according to Rosa, had considered a rather strange present for a woman of eighty. When Harriet told the birthday girl this she laughed delightedly.

'Men! Allegra chose well. I see no reason why age should prevent me from pampering my skin.'

The rest of the day passed swiftly. Harriet was admitted to the large kitchen, where a crowd of voluble women gave the visitor a warm welcome as they began on the final preparations. Harriet helped lay a vast, damask cloth on the long table in the dining room, then began fashioning the matching napkins into lily and rosebud shapes which won the extravagant admiration of Silvia and her crew as they stacked plates and silverware at one end of the table, to leave room for the great platters of food they had taken days to prepare for the event.

And when floral birthday tributes arrived for Signora Fortinari at regular intervals, Harriet won everyone's gratitude by arranging them in artistic displays to decorate the salon and the hall, and as a spectacular centrepiece for the table.

Because the day was warm enough to eat lunch out on the loggia Harriet insisted on serving it there herself to free Silvia for more pressing duties.

'You have changed so much, Rosa,' said Vittoria Fortinari, leaning back in a cane chair as she smiled at Harriet.

'I've grown up,' said Harriet soberly. Which was true enough, of both Rosa and herself. In different ways very difficult as teenagers, she felt that both of them had grown into women with more responsibility and gravitas than either of their families had ever dared hope at one time. She paused in the act of pouring coffee, seized by a sudden surge of anticipation as she heard an engine growling up the bends of the road towards the villa.

'Dante!' said the signora, to Harriet's disappointment. Vittoria Fortinari beamed as a scarlet motor cycle streaked perilously through the stone pillars below and roared up the garden to come to a spectacular halt at the foot of the stone steps. A smaller, younger, and more beautiful version of Leo vaulted from it and ran up the stairs towards them, stopping in front of the signora with a low, flourishing bow, before seizing her in his arms and giving her a resounding kiss on both cheeks.

'Happy birthday, Nonna,' he said, in lighter, more musical tones than his brother, then turned to eye Harriet with open appreciation. 'And this, of course, is the famous Rosa!'

Harriet was beginning to think that Rosa had been dangerously economical with the details of her youthful transgression. For a moment she eyed the slim figure in black leather quizzically, then gave him a friendly smile and held out her hand.

'And this is the famous Dante.'

Dante laughed delightedly, took the hand in his and kissed her on both cheeks. 'You were only ten when I saw you last, Rosa,' he said, eyes dancing. 'You were all eyes and braids. And permanently in trouble.'

'Not any more,' she assured him. At least, not if she could possibly help it.

'Leo said I should wait until tonight to meet you again,' he said cheerfully, 'but I was impatient to see if you had improved since I saw you last, Rosa. And you have!'

'Many thanks,' said Harriet dryly.

'Impudent boy,' said his grandmother lovingly. 'Sit down and drink some coffee.'

'In a moment,' he promised, and went back down to the Ducati. He took a parcel from the pannier, then raced up the steps and went down on one knee in front of his grandmother. 'For the love of my life,' he said theatrically, and handed the present over.

His grandmother tapped his cheek, laughing, then gave him a kiss and told him to get up and sit beside Rosa while she unwrapped her present. Both women exclaimed in delight as she took out a black velvet stole lined with red silk, and Signora Fortinari got up at once to take it to her room before anything could spoil it.

'So, Rosa, how are you enjoying your return to the fold?' asked Dante without preamble, his dark eyes so obviously free of malice Harriet relaxed.

'Very much. So far.'

'Forgive my absence at dinner last night. Leo sent me off on an errand to keep me out of the way.' Dante grinned. 'And having met you again I can see why! He wanted you to himself.'

'I hardly think so,' said Harriet, flushing.

Dante shook his dark, glossy head. 'If you mean all that old history, forget it, Rosa. Everyone else has.'

'You weren't here at the time,' she reminded him.

'No,' he said regretfully. 'I was visiting friends in Napa Valley, in California. I missed all the fun. But I heard all about it when I got back.'

'I'm glad it gave everyone so much entertainment,' said Harriet stiffly and Dante shook his head, abruptly serious.

'Leo told only me, Rosa, because I came back just after you'd been sent home, and plagued him to tell me why he had a black eye. But otherwise the only one who knows what really happened, except Leo and Nonna, is Guido Bracco, of course. And *he* won't be here tonight. He lives in New York now.'

Something for which Harriet was profoundly grateful. Rosa had made no mention of Guido Bracco. Nor of Leo's black eye.

When his grandmother came back to join them Dante chatted amiably for a while then took his leave.

'You must rest, Nonna, to look more beautiful than ever tonight, then we shall all come back this evening to help you celebrate.'

Harriet stood with Vittoria Fortinari to wave as Dante kicked the Ducati into life and took off with the panache typical of his age and race.

'Leave the coffee tray, Rosa,' said Vittoria. 'I must go up for my rest now, but first I want to see the dresses you brought.'

'I hope my room's tidy enough for you,' joked Harriet, as they reached Rosa's bedroom.

'It is immaculate, darling!' said Signora Fortinari, looking round. She sighed, her face falling into sudden lines. 'When you were young I had to lecture you to keep your room tidy. But I shall never lecture you again.'

'Which dress do you prefer, Nonna?' said Harriet swiftly to divert her.

The signora brightened as Harriet held up each dress in turn. One was long and narrow, in bronze double chiffon, with a deep V-shaped neckline held up by a handful of thin, satin strands on each shoulder. The other was a short, strapless sheath in stretchy black crepe, embroidered here and there with sprays of raised silk flowers.

'They are both beautiful, darling!' Vittoria gazed at each in turn, then back to Harriet. 'I cannot decide.'

'Are *you* wearing a long dress, Nonna?'

'Yes. Black velvet, as Dante obviously knew, clever boy.'

'Then I'll wear a long one, too,' said Harriet, preferring the bronze chiffon because it covered more and clung less than the tube dress.

After Signora Fortinari had retired to her room to rest Harriet took a book down to the loggia, stretched out on a cane sofa, stuffed some cushions beneath her head and settled down to read, determined not to worry any more about what the evening might bring. So far no one in the family had unmasked her as an impostor, so it seemed unlikely anyone else would, either. Harriet smiled to herself at the melodrama of the idea, and settled down to enjoy the intricate plot, soon so involved that she failed to respond when someone called Rosa's name.

Alerted by a shadow on the page, she looked up to see Leonardo Fortinari gazing down at her, a smile playing at the corners of his mouth.

'It must be a very good book. I called your name twice.'

Rosa's name. She must be more careful.

Smiling brightly, Harriet showed him the author's photograph on the flyleaf. 'She's my favourite crime writer—I was lost to the world. Nonna's resting in her room,' she added. 'Did you want her?'

'Not at the moment,' said Leo, and reached down to swing her legs to the floor so that he could sit beside her. 'I want you.'

Harriet jerked upright, making much show of arranging cushions. 'What can I do for you?'

'If I told you,' he said, in a tone that sent colour rushing to her face. 'You might blush even more deeply, little cousin.'

'Leo, I don't trust you in this mood,' said Harriet suspiciously. 'You were anything but friendly when I arrived. Why the change?'

He took her hand in his, and began smoothing a finger over it. 'I was still thinking of Rosa as she was. But when I had time to observe you with Nonna, so much warmer and loving towards her, I saw you with new eyes. Rosa the woman, instead of the baby siren who miscalculated her knowledge of men so badly.'

Heavens, thought Harriet with foreboding. What exactly had Rosa been *up* to all those years ago?

'It's a long time ago. People change,' she said shortly, and detached her hand. 'Dante came here earlier.'

'I know. He told me.' Leo locked his eyes with hers. 'I forbid you to encourage Dante. If you practice your wiles on anyone, choose me. I am familiar with them, remember.'

For a moment Harriet thought her Italian vocabulary had let her down. 'Did I actually hear you say forbid?' she demanded.

'Yes, Rosa. You did.'

Her eyes flashed angrily. 'I came here for Nonna's sake. Not to see you, nor to seduce Dante. Nor anyone else. I do have a life, Leo. Even though you've done your best to spoil it by influencing Nonna against me all these years. She admitted as much to me last night.'

'I was determined to shield her from further hurt,' he said curtly.

'I doubt it was just that,' said Harriet scornfully.

'Tell the truth, Leo. You wanted me to suffer for my sins.'

'I had my reasons. And you know them all!' he cut back.

If only she did, thought Harriet, so startled by a sudden, overpowering urge to kiss the pulse throbbing beside his mouth she jumped to her feet.

Leo followed suit, barring her way into the house. 'Rosa—'

'Please,' said Harriet breathlessly. 'It's Nonna's birthday. I don't want to fight with you, Leo.'

His gave her a deeply unsettling smile. 'I have no wish to *fight*, Rosa—I want to make love to you.'

Harriet gazed up at him, mesmerised for a moment by the look in Leo Fortinari's eyes. Then she turned away sharply. He hadn't returned Rosa's youthful passion, she reminded herself, so why the change towards her? But then, she wasn't Rosa. She was someone Leo had no idea he'd never met until twenty four hours ago.

'As I keep saying,' she informed him, ignoring her racing pulse, 'I've changed, Leo. Whatever unwelcome attentions I embarrassed you with in the past I've no intention of repeating them.'

'Even if I made it clear that this time I would welcome them?' he said, coming closer.

Harriet turned to face him. 'Why are you doing this, Leo? Is it out of revenge because I was a nuisance once?'

Leo laughed shortly. 'No, Rosa. Not because you were a *nuisance*.' He seized her by the elbows, his touch burning through the fine wool of her sweater. 'It is not an emotion familiar to me, but perhaps I was jealous.'

Harriet stared up at him, her mind working furiously. Had he found out about Pascal Tavernier?

Leo shrugged. 'All women like Dante.'

'I can see why,' Harriet agreed, pulling away. 'He's very good looking.'

'I know it. And charming, and good-tempered—all those things I am not.' Leo smiled crookedly. 'None of this worries me, you understand. What does worry me is that my brother found our little cousin so delectable.'

'Is that why you sent him to Arezzo today—to save him from the dangerous Rosa?' she said with sarcasm.

Leo nodded. 'I asked him to fetch the gift I'd ordered for Nonna. I told him I was too busy to go myself.'

Harriet looked at him in silence for a moment. 'You were wrong about one thing, Leo.'

'What is it?'

'Dante's more charming and a *lot* less domineering,' she said, throwing caution to the winds. 'But you're wrong about the looks.'

With a sudden, smothered exclamation Harriet's Italian didn't cover, Leo took her in his arms and kissed her mouth. Her lips parted with such involuntary response that Leo sat down abruptly, pulling her onto his lap. He slid his hands into her hair and held her face immobile as he kissed her, and Harriet responded mindlessly for a moment, until a hard, unmistakable pressure beneath her thighs brought her off his lap so suddenly she stumbled as she backed away, her colour high, conscious, too late, that it was broad daylight, and interruption was likely any moment.

Leo rose slowly to his feet, breathing hard, but

making no attempt to hide his formidable arousal. 'Do you want me to apologize?'

She shook her head, scarlet to the roots of her hair. 'I could have said no.'

'But you did not.' He moved nearer. 'Could it be that whatever attraction I had for you once still exists?'

'*No,*' said Harriet, in an effort to keep Rosa out of trouble.

'No?' Leo smiled, his eyes gleaming with indulgent disbelief. 'We shall see,' he promised, in a tone which triggered alarm bells in Harriet's brain. Then he turned, smiling, as his grandmother came out to join them.

'Nonna, I came to wish you happy birthday.'

Signora Fortinari embraced him warmly as he kissed her. 'I thought I heard your voice, Leo. Why did you trouble to come this afternoon when you will be seeing me tonight?'

'I couldn't allow Dante to shame me by his attentions,' he assured her, with a gleaming look at Harriet.

'You are very good to me, both of you,' said Vittoria, patting his cheek, then she turned to Harriet. 'And have you had a restful afternoon, darling?'

'I read for a while, then Leo came,' said Harriet. And Leo Fortinari could be described in many ways, but restful wasn't one of them.

'Now we shall have some English tea,' said his grandmother decisively. 'Will you stay, Leo?'

'I would like to above all things, Nonna, but I have a lot to do. I shall see you both later.' Leo kissed his grandmother on both cheeks. 'Shall I order your tea for you?'

'No, darling, I'd better talk to Silvia myself for a

moment, make sure all is well for tonight.' Signora Fortinari gave them both an indulgent smile, then left them alone.

'Until tonight, then, Rosa.' Leo seized Harriet in his arms and kissed her swiftly. 'Do not encourage Dante,' he said against her mouth, then ruffled her hair with a negligent hand, and went down the steps to his car. As he opened the door he looked up at her. 'Nor anyone else,' he warned, with a glittering look which warned Harriet that she would need all her wits about her to avoid presenting Rosa Mostyn with a problem neither of them had foreseen.

CHAPTER FOUR

HARRIET STUDIED HER REFLECTION later, feeling like an actress about to give the performance of her life. Tonight, in her expensive borrowed plumes, she could almost believe she *was* Rosa. The dress was long and narrow, with a neckline cut to show a subtle hint of cleavage, the handful of fine satin straps at the shoulders Harriet's only ornament other than the borrowed ring, and a pair of pendant pearl earrings once given to Rosa's mother by Signora Fortinari.

Harriet smiled wryly at her reflection. 'Come on then, Rosa-Cinderella. Time for the party.'

Only it wasn't just a party, but a daunting test of Harriet Foster's memory and acting abilities. Leo Fortinari was the biggest, and most unexpected problem. Rosa had strongly advised a cool, distant attitude towards her cousin, never dreaming that in Leo Harriet would find a lover who, with only a touch of his lips and hands, would teach her, at last, about sexual arousal. Guy Warren had regularly complained that Harriet's sultry looks were totally at odds with her cool self-control. As others had done before him. But now, for the first time in her life, and at exactly the wrong time and with the wrong man, Harriet had proved them wrong. Or Leo had. Which meant, she reminded herself stringently, that she must never forget that Leo Fortinari was dangerous not only because of his unexpected effect on her, but his inside knowledge of Rosa's fall from grace. Harriet felt a trickle of apprehension. It was obvious, now, that Rosa had omitted certain details. While Leo knew every last one.

Feeling that she was treading a tightrope through a minefield, Harriet went downstairs slowly to find Leo Fortinari watching her from below.

'Good evening, Rosa,' he said huskily, giving her a smile which made her tremble inside. 'You are utterly ravishing tonight.'

So are you, she thought despairingly. He wore a dark suit of impeccable cut, his shirt gleamed white against his olive skin, and to Harriet he was everything she'd ever dreamed of in a man.

'You're early, Leo,' she said quietly, trying to control her racing pulse.

'I wanted a few moments alone with you before the others arrive.' He took her hand to draw her outside onto the loggia. 'Nonna will not be down for a while yet.'

'How do you know?'

'I checked with Silvia.' He kept her hand in his and drew her close beside him, his thigh brushing hers through the featherweight fabric of the dress. 'Rosa, this is not what I intended,' he said abruptly, staring at the view.

'You meant to come later?' she parried.

Leo turned his head to look down into her upturned face. 'I meant, Rosa, that when I heard you were coming back I had no intention of letting you work your wiles on me again. You are no longer a child,' he added, with a twist to his mouth. 'We are both very different from the Leo and Rosa of the last time you were here.'

More than you know, thought Harriet ruefully,

wondering where this was leading. 'I thought you'd have been married by now.'

'As I should have been,' Leo agreed. 'But Luisa Bracco put an end to the engagement after I thrashed her brother—but you know all this, Rosa,' he added impatiently.

Rosa, Rosa, what were you *up* to? thought Harriet wildly. This Guido Bracco, who was in New York now, had obviously been Rosa's choice to make Leo jealous all those years ago. But Rosa had never mentioned him, nor his sister.

Harriet eyed the acquiline profile thoughtfully, wondering if Leo still languished over the unknown Luisa. 'I'm sorry. Did you love her very much?'

He smiled a little. 'Her family owns vineyards that adjoin ours. It would have been a suitable marriage.'

'Suitable?' Harriet stared. 'Is that all you expect from marriage?'

Leo shrugged. 'Luisa was—is—a beautiful woman. It would have been no hardship to play the husband. We had known each other all our lives, remember.'

'Where is she now?' asked Harriet, praying that Luisa was safely in New York with her brother.

Leo's grasp tightened as he smiled down at her. 'At this precise moment I imagine Luisa is in a car with her sister Sophia, on the way here to the Villa Castiglione, to celebrate Nonna's birthday.'

Harriet stared at him in horror. 'No! Please say you're joking.'

Leo laughed indulgently. 'Don't be afraid, Rosa. I will protect you.'

'Thanks a lot! Is she married to someone else now?'

'She was. She is a widow now. You must have heard about it.'

'If I did, I've forgotten,' said Harriet firmly.

Just say you've forgotten, Rosa had instructed. Nine years is a long time. No one will expect Rosa Mostyn to remember everything.

'After I got back my father preferred to forget I'd ever been to Tuscany that year, and Mother was discouraged from passing on any family news,' said Harriet, reporting Rosa's bitterness on the subject.

'And so your father sent you to work in the kitchens of the Hermitage,' commented Leo. 'A touch of the medieval about your penance, Rosa. Did you object?'

'Yes, of course,' said Harriet impatiently. 'But only because it happened at that particular point. Little Rosa was always destined for the family business. Tony had to start in the same way. Only he went to college first. I was made to reverse the process and go to college later.' She turned away, trying to detach her hand, but Leo held on to it, his fingers stroking her skin. 'Surely there have been other women in your life since Luisa Bracco?' she couldn't help asking.

'Of course, Rosa. I am no monk. But neither have I found anyone I wish to marry. Not that this matters. Dante will provide a Fortinari heir one day.'

'Surely you want children yourself?'

'Only if I meet a woman I consider 'suitable' for their mother,' Leo mocked, and pulled on her hand, drawing her round to face him. 'Do you want children, Rosa?'

'Yes,' said Harriet on Rosa's behalf, then realized with a jolt that she was also speaking for herself. Up to now the only children she had ever thought about were the ones she taught. But now... She looked up into Leo's intent eyes, only half aware of the noise and activity coming from somewhere in the house, as the last of the preparations were made. 'It's time we went in,' she said abruptly. Before she did something *really* stupid, and blotted Rosa's copybook forever.

'As you wish,' said Leo, touching a hand to her hair. 'Have no fear, Rosa. I shall not spoil such perfection by making love to you. At least not now. Not here.'

Harriet took in a deep breath. 'Leo, you're not going to make love to me at all. Anywhere. I'm not the girl you used to know. Believe me.'

'I do believe you,' he said, moving close enough for her to feel his breath on her cheek. 'You are very different—no longer a headstrong child, but a mature, beautiful woman. A woman I yearn to seize in my arms and kiss until she begs for mercy.'

Monday, thought Harriet, closing her eyes in desperation. All I have to do is get through tonight and tomorrow and then Monday I can go home. Back to Pennington where I belong.

Leo released her hand reluctantly as the drone of car engines sounded on the climb to the villa. 'We shall talk later,' he promised. 'In the meantime let us find Nonna and tell her the first guests are almost here.'

There was just time for mutual admiration as Vittoria Fortinari came down the stairs, resplendent in a black velvet gown, with Dante's dramatic scarf draped round her shoulders. She exclaimed as she saw Harriet, and as predicted, took due note of the earrings she'd once given Rosa's mother.

'You look breathtaking, my child. You agree,

Leo?' she asked her grandson, who nodded his dark head gravely.

'That is precisely the word for her.' He bent low over his grandmother's hand. 'While you, Nonna look superb. Will you wear this tonight, with my love?' He handed her a gold chain with a tiny diamond pendant in the shape of a V.

His grandmother exclaimed in rapture at the sight of it, and kissed Leo lovingly, then bent her head so that he could fasten it round her neck.

'Perfect,' said Harriet, viewing the effect, and Vittoria Fortinari smiled at them radiantly.

'As you say, Rosa, perfect. I am a fortunate woman tonight. Come. We shall stand together in the the hall, the three of us, as we greet the guests. And you, Leo, can supply Rosa with any names she may not recall.'

'That,' he said, with a smile at Harriet, 'is the other reason why I came early.'

It was an arrangement which made things surprisingly easy. With Leo to whisper in her ear as people approached, or an introduction by Signora Fortinari to friends Rosa wouldn't have met before, the first part of the evening went off far more smoothly than Harriet had dared hope. Dante was the first to come hurrying into the hall, followed by a fair young man with a pretty girl in a maternity dress which identified her as Mirella. There was much kissing and embracing, an introduction to Franco Paglia, Mirella's husband, then people began arriving quickly, Silvia and her cohorts appeared with trays of drinks, and suddenly the party was in full swing. Harriet accepted a glass of champagne and was just congratulating herself that she'd rubbed through the ordeal fairly well, when Leo whispered in her ear.

'The last of the guests are arriving. Sophia Bracco and her husband Marco Rossi. But no Luisa.'

Harriet sent up a fervent prayer of thanks and braced herself, grateful for Leo's presence beside her as a statuesque blond woman sailed into the crowded hall, with a distinguished, grey-haired man following in her wake. Sophia Rossi had hair of a miraculous gold shade, and voluptuous curves swathed in low-cut black chiffon chosen, it was obvious, as a backdrop for the magnificent diamonds she wore in her ears, round her throat and wrists, and on several of her fingers.

Signora Fortinari welcomed them both, exchanged kisses with Sophia, who made apologies for her sister, who was unwell. Sophia turned to Leo with a dazzling smile and embraced him warmly, but he detached himself to draw Harriet forward.

'You remember Sophia, of course, Rosa. But let me present you to her husband, Marco Rossi.'

Marco Rossi was at least twenty years older than his wife, and a man Harriet liked on sight. His shrewd blue eyes twinkled as he bowed over her hand, and told her their meeting was a pleasure he had long anticipated.

'You are much changed, Rosa,' said Sophia coolly, looking Harriet up and down.

'So are you, Sophia,' returned Harriet. 'I hardly recognized you.'

To her astonishment she met a blaze of pure rage in the other woman's eyes. Dante intervened hastily, saying he was taking Rosa away to play with people her own age, a pleasantry which found no favour at all with Sophia Rossi, nor, Harriet saw, looking back as Dante towed her away, with Leo Fortinari.

'I shall come and rescue you very soon, Rosa,' Leo promised her, oblivious to the glare Sophia gave him, or Marco Rossi's wry amusement.

Dante was chortling as he took Harriet to join Mirella and Franco in the salon. 'Rosa has just made an enemy,' he explained.

'If you mean Sophia Bracco,' said Harriet, taking the bull by the horns, 'I'm afraid I did that years ago.'

'Don't mind Sophia,' said Mirella comfortably, and moved up on the sofa so that Harriet could sit down.

'What happened?' asked Franco, who was a very friendly young man, and very obviously anxious about his wife. 'Would you like a cushion, my darling?'

'No,' said Mirella, laughing. 'As it is I'm conspicuous as the only person made to sit down. It's kind of you to keep me company, Rosa.'

'I'm glad to in these heels,' said Harriet with truth, then smiled ruefully at Franco. 'I thought everyone knew that when I was very young and very silly I tried to make Leo jealous with Sophia's brother Guido,' she said bluntly.

'Bad choice.' Dante pulled a face as he leaned over the back of the sofa. 'Guido responded with too much enthusiasm and scared little Rosa half to death, at which point Leo found them and beat Guido up for daring to take liberties with Leo Fortinari's cousin. Luisa Bracco was so incensed about the punishment Leo gave her amorous fool of a brother, she gave the ring back. Great mistake, because Leo—being Leo—thanked her politely and kept it.'

Harriet controlled a shudder. No wonder Rosa had skimped on the details. 'Sophia obviously still feels hostile towards me. She gave me a killing look just as Dante arrived to save the day.'

'Ah, that was because you said you hardly recognized her,' said Dante, grinning. 'Last time you saw Sophia she was several kilos lighter—unlike her hair, which was dark.'

Mirella chuckled. 'A good thing she married Marco Rossi. He's rich enough to let her spend a fortune on her hair and clothes.'

'And her jewellery, by the look of those diamonds,' said Franco, then bent to help his wife to her feet. 'Time for supper.'

Dante, outrageous in a black velvet suit and a ruffled black silk shirt, offered his arm to Harriet. 'Come on then, little cousin. Let us eat before Sophia casts a spell and turns the food to ashes.'

'You don't like her?' said Harriet curiously, as they followed the others to the dining room.

'No,' said Dante baldly. 'I didn't like Luisa, either. Leo was furious with you at the time, but in my opinion he should be grateful to you for saving him from a horrible fate. Though since you came back to us,' he added, grinning at Leo as he came to join them, 'I think he is.'

'What are you talking about, Dante?' demanded his brother.

'We were telling Franco what happened last time Rosa was here.'

Leo gave his brother an annihilating glare. 'Which is best forgotten,' he snapped. 'Besides, only Rosa and I know what really happened,' he added, with a glance at Harriet which turned her blood cold.

She shivered. There was obviously more to it than Dante knew. And it was becoming more obvious by the minute that Rosa hadn't dared volunteer the whole truth in case Harriet refused to make the trip.

'Don't look so tragic,' Leo said very quietly. 'Forget the past and concentrate on the present. Tonight is a night to celebrate.'

'Amen to that,' said Dante in relief, and flanked by the Fortinari brothers Harriet went in to supper with Mirella and Franco, the four of them staying close beside her as the other guests exclaimed at the beauty of the table and the wonderful array of food. Leo sent Dante off to see that his grandmother lacked nothing, then suggested they ate their supper on the loggia.

'No, Rosa,' he said imperiously, as Harriet moved to take a plate. 'You and Mirella go outside and find chairs. Franco and I will choose for you.'

Outside in the loggia, which had been strung with lanterns to augment the moonlight, Mirella sank into a chair gratefully. 'I can't stand about much these days.'

Harriet leaned against the balustrade beside her. 'When is the baby due?'

'Christmas Day—the perfect gift. I can't wait to hold my child in my arms.' Mirella looked up at her curiously. 'Tell me about yourself, Rosa. Is there someone you want to marry?'

'Maybe,' hedged Harriet, thinking of Pascal Tavernier.

Mirella smiled, and instead of pressing for details, began talking of Signora Fortinari's joy in having Rosa back with her again.

'We are all glad,' declared Dante, joining them with the others. 'Franco has given you a very meagre supper, Mirella. Is your bridegroom starving you?'

Franco gave Dante a boisterous shove which resulted in some juggling with the plates of food, and under cover of the uproar Leo handed Rosa a plate, and unfurled a lily-shaped napkin to place in her lap.

'In case these idiots ruin that dress,' he said scathingly as he took his place beside Harriet.

'Do you like it?' she asked, then felt her face suffuse with colour as Leo gave her a slow, comprehensive survey much enjoyed by the others.

'We all like it,' Dante assured her. 'You are a vision to behold, Rosa.'

'Which obviously added to Sophia's fury,' said Mirella, with a giggle she hastily changed to a cough as the lady in question came outside to join them, escorted by her husband.

'We thought we'd find you out here,' said Sophia, smiling at Leo. 'It's so hot inside we shall join you. Marco, fetch a chair for me.'

Harriet looked on in amusement as Sophia Rossi pulled her chair close to Leo, blatant in her aim to divert his attention from his cousin. Her husband joined Harriet, and courteously engaged her in conversation, but the moment Sophia noticed his absorption she launched into questions about the recent Fortinari vintage to make the conversation general.

Leo responded politely, but Dante interrupted with humorous complaints about the long hours his slave-driver brother forced him to work until the grapes were safely harvested.

'Leo works far longer hours than you do,' said Mirella, surrendering her half-empty plate to her anxious husband.

'You're not hungry, darling?'

'No room for more,' she said apologetically, and gave an admonishing look at Dante. 'You see? That's why Franco didn't heap my plate as high as yours, greedy one.'

'Sophia was the same when she was expecting our son,' said Marco comfortably.

'I'm sure no one wants to hear about that,' snapped his wife, and demanded to know who Signora Fortinari had hired to do the flowers. 'Such exquisite arrangements,' she gushed, leaning across Harriet to give Marco her empty plate. 'I must engage the same firm for my next party.'

'Rosa did them,' said Leo, in a tone which told Harriet he was trying not to laugh.

'Did you really, Rosa?' said Mirella, impressed. 'How clever you are.'

'Part of your hotel training, I suppose,' said Sophia with a sniff, obviously furious she'd ever mentioned flowers. She turned her back on Harriet and held out her glass to Leo. 'Could I have some wine, please?'

The red wine they were drinking was of a quality Marco Rossi commented on with appreciation as he touched his glass to Harriet's.

'I shall buy more of this, Leo,' he said genially. 'Potent and heady, but very smooth.'

Rather like Leo, thought Harriet, sipping cautiously, then gasped as Sophia got up suddenly, and in the process managed to spill the entire contents of her glass down Rosa Mostyn's expensive dress.

At once there was uproar as everyone exclaimed in horror, and Dante and Leo sprang to supply napkins to blot the stain.

'You must take it off at once, Rosa,' said Mirella in distress. 'Such a beautiful dress—perhaps cold water?'

'I'm *so* sorry,' said Sophia, with patent insincerity.

'But if it is spoiled, no matter, Marco will pay for another.'

'Unnecessary,' said Harriet tightly, yearning to punch Sophia Rossi on the nose.

'But I insist,' said Marco Rossi, with a look at his wife which visibly subdued her. 'It was my wife's fault, so please allow me to replace the dress, Miss Rosa.'

'Unnecessary, Marco,' said Leo coldly. 'I shall do that.'

Dante leapt into the breach quickly. 'Hurry upstairs and change quickly, Rosa, before Nonna notices. We shan't mind if you come back in your jeans.'

'Such a fuss,' complained Sophia petulantly.

Leo Fortinari gave her a look which made her quail. 'We want nothing to spoil my grandmother's birthday.'

'Come,' said Marco Rossi, taking his wife by the arm, 'let us try to be good guests and circulate, my dear.'

Glad that Signora Fortinari was absorbed with a circle of friends in the salon, Harriet took off her shoes and sprinted up the stairs undetected, secretly devastated by the ruin of a dress more beautiful than anything she'd ever worn. Inside her room she stripped it off to find the stain had spread through everything she had on. Cursing Sophia Rossi, with no time for a shower Harriet sponged herself down, found fresh underwear, then pulled on the black tube dress. Sophia might have it in for Rosa, but if she imagined she'd routed her she was wrong, thought Harriet militantly, as she pulled the stretchy fabric into place across her breasts. The dress stopped short at her knees, left her shoulders bare, and clung so lovingly to every curve in between Harriet whistled silently at her reflection, brushed her hair, touched up her make-up, then went to the door to find Leo outside, waiting for her.

'Merciful God,' he said involuntarily at the sight of her. 'Take care you keep far away from Sophia. One look at that dress and she will stab you with one of Nonna's table knives.'

'It was the only alternative,' said Harriet defensively. 'If I came down in jeans Sophia would have won.'

'Instead of which, victory is most definitely yours, Rosa. In every way,' he added, his voice deepening in a way which made her back away instinctively.

'We must go down,' she said quickly. 'Before Nonna misses me.'

'She already has. I explained that you'd spilt wine on your dress and needed to change.' Leo fell in step with her as they went downstairs. 'I made no mention of Sophia.'

'Good.' Harriet glanced at him. 'She really detests me, doesn't she! She must have been very fond of her brother and sister. Though she obviously holds no grudge against you,' she added, slyly.

Leo paused at the foot of the stairs. 'You have no idea at all why she dislikes you, Rosa?'

'An idea, yes,' said Harriet cautiously. 'But that's all.'

'I will explain. Later,' promised Leo, then took her by the hand and led her into the salon, where Signora Fortinari was holding court with Dante, Mirella and Franco close at hand.

'Rosa,' she said, beckoning. 'Such a shame about

your dress.' Then she smiled mischievously. 'Though the replacement is hardly a disappointment.'

There was a ripple of appreciative laughter among her friends, then Mirella kissed her grandmother good-night, slipped one arm through Harriet's, the other through Franco's and asked her brothers to see them off.

'I want to say my good-nights to the others,' said Mirella with anticipation.

'You mean you want to watch Sophia's face when she sees Rosa's dress!' said her husband.

'Don't we all!' said Dante, laughing, and Leo shook his head at him with mock severity.

'Behave, you two. Marco is a valued client, remember. Also,' he added, 'I like him very much.'

'So do I,' agreed Dante. 'Poor man. Imagine being married to Sophia!'

'Stop it,' hissed Mirella, as they went into the dining room.

The Rossis were at the far end, where Sophia was queening it among some of her own social circle as Mirella and Franco approached to say their goodbyes. She turned, smiling, to say good-night to Mirella, then stopped mid-sentence, her smile frozen on her lips as she caught sight of Harriet.

Marco Rossi's eyes twinkled appreciatively. 'You were remarkably swift in providing a new dress, Leo. And such a dress, if I may say so, Miss Rosa.'

Harriet felt almost sorry for Sophia Rossi. For a fleeting moment the other woman looked stricken, but she rallied quickly, made some flippant remark about Rosa's forethought in bringing two dresses, then she turned to her husband with a feverishly bright smile and said she was ready to go home.

Once Mirella and Franco were seen to their car, and the Rossis had departed, Dante drew Harriet into a group of friends far more welcoming than Sophia, while Leo went off to talk to his grandmother.

For a while Harriet managed to chat easily, but though Dante was good company, and the other guests careful to include her in their conversation, she was only happy again when Leo rejoined her. I missed him, she thought, dismayed. Which is madness. Get a grip, Harriet Foster. Just another day, then Monday you fly home.

'Is everything well with you?' asked Leo in an undertone.

'Very well. How is Nonna bearing up? Is she tired?'

'Another half hour, she insists, so in a while Dante and I will ask Silvia to bring in coffee, and after that everyone will pay their respects and go home.'

The house was quiet after Signora Fortinari had talked about the success of the party for a while, kissed Harriet and her grandsons good-night, then retired happily to her room.

'You go on, Dante,' ordered Leo. 'I will follow.'

For a moment Dante looked rebellious, but at a look from his brother he smiled philosophically at Harriet, kissed her warmly on both cheeks and left them alone.

'Are you very tired?' asked Leo.

They were standing in the hall, where they'd watched Signora Fortinari out of sight as she went up to bed.

'A little,' said Harriet. In actual fact she felt exhausted, but had no intention of admitting it in case Leo felt he should leave immediately.

But Leo made it plain he had no intention of leaving. He took her into the salon, and closed the door firmly behind him. Then he drew Harriet down beside him on the velvet sofa, smiling wryly at the apprehensive look in her eyes.

'Rosa, I want only to talk to you,' he reassured her. 'I will not deny that I also want to make love to you. But this is my grandmother's house, and you and I have caused her far too much trouble in the past to risk causing more.'

Harriet relaxed slightly. 'So what did you want to talk about?'

Leo kept her hand in his, looking at her in silence for a moment. 'I thought you might be curious as to why, even after all these years, Sophia feels such animosity towards you.'

'I assumed it was the beating you gave her brother.'

'It is part of it,' he agreed. He smiled wryly. 'But she blames you for much more than that.'

Harriet shook her head with sudden violence, wanting to run away and hide rather than hear the truth. 'Please, Leo. Let's not rake up the past any more.'

He turned to look at her. 'Aren't you curious to know why Sophia resents you enough to ruin your dress?'

'I already know why, Leo. Sophia obviously lusts after you.' Harriet looked at him squarely. 'And for some reason imagines you lust after me.'

His eyes lit with sudden, explicit heat. 'And she is right. I do.'

CHAPTER FIVE

HYPNOTISED BY THE black, compelling gaze, Harriet felt limp with relief when Leo broke the tense silence at last.

'You know very well that I find you desirable, Rosa, now that you are a woman. But—'

'But you didn't when I was a silly teenager,' Harriet finished for him.

Leo shrugged. 'Nevertheless, Sophia believed I did. When Luisa ended the engagement Sophia offered herself to me in exchange. She was quite unconcerned about my treatment of her brother, even grateful for it, she informed me, since it made Luisa so angry. Apparently Sophia had always been convinced that my engagement to her sister was purely a matter of convenience to please our fathers, and truly believed that all along I had really wanted her instead. When I explained, as gently as I could, that she was mistaken, she had hysterics and accused me of coveting you and the Mostyn money more than her share of the Bracco vineyards. Nothing I could say would convince her this was untrue. Soon afterwards she married Marco Rossi, and since then we meet only at occasions like this.'

Harriet let out a deep breath. 'I suppose I'm lucky it was only wine she threw at me.'

Leo's jaw tightened. 'I had no idea she would do anything so outrageous. But Nonna insisted we invite

Luisa and the Rossis, to show the world the old enmity no longer existed.'

'I can only feel glad that Luisa didn't show up,' said Harriet with feeling, but Leo shook his head.

'Luisa is very different from Sophia, and far too dignified to make a scene in public. She gave ill health as her excuse, but I believe she thought it best to stay away tonight.'

For which Harriet was deeply grateful. 'Thank you for explaining, Leo. Would you think me very rude if I said I was tired and need to go to bed?'

'Of course not.' Leo stood up, holding out his hand to pull her to her feet, then frowned. 'Strange. I had remembered you as taller.'

He was right. One of the few discrepancies between Harriet and Rosa was a difference of three inches in height.

'It's a long time since you've seen me,' she said lightly, then caught her breath at the look in his eyes.

'Too long,' he agreed softly. 'Now we are together again it is time I apologised for my part in keeping you and Nonna from each other.'

'It's not only your fault,' she said, remembering Rosa's regrets. 'All I had to do was tell Nonna how sorry I was, but as time went on it grew harder. Especially as my father discouraged my mother's efforts to mend the rift.'

'Perhaps your father thought the Fortinaris should have taken better care of his daughter,' said Leo soberly.

'Rebellious teenage girls tend to be hard to take care of,' said Harriet, remembering her own adolescence.

'Nevertheless, when I discovered you with Guido

I was enraged that he could dare to treat a relative of mine in such a way. He was lucky I didn't murder him!'

Harriet stepped back involuntarily. 'Please, Leo. Let's forget all that now.'

Leo gazed down at her, an expression on his handsome face she recognized a split second too late. By then she was in his arms and his mouth was on hers and she was lost. If he'd used his not inconsiderable strength to get his way she might have struggled, but in response to his slow, inflammatory kisses Harriet responded helplessly to his seeking tongue as he drew her up on tiptoe, his caressing hand smoothing her body against his.

As she felt the pressure of his arousal Harriet trembled and he picked her up and sat down with her in his lap.

'Can you feel how much I want you?' he said hoarsely, and pulled the dress down so he could bury his face against her naked breasts. Harriet shivered uncontrollably, her heart thudding as she felt his skilled fingers and seeking mouth on wanton nipples which sprang erect in response. Her body vibrated with sensations she had never dreamed of as his caresses roused her to fever pitch, and at last Leo raised his head, the searching look in his eyes strangely at odds with his ragged breathing. 'Rosa?'

Harriet's heat and desire evaporated abruptly. She pushed him away and stood up, tugging her dress into place. He wanted Rosa, not Harriet Foster, she reminded herself viciously, her colour high as she avoided his eyes. Leo got slowly to his feet and grasped her face with an ungentle hand.

'Is this punishment? Retribution for my indifference all those years ago?'

'No,' she said flatly, somehow managing to look at him with defiance, instead of throwing herself into his arms. 'It's the Brit in me preaching common sense.'

His hot urgency cooled visibly. 'How greatly you have changed,' he said. 'Young Rosa was a stranger to common sense.'

'Not an attribute teenagers are famous for.'

'True.' Leo looked at her quizzically. 'So. I must kiss only your hand and say good night. Is that what you want, Rosa?'

'You said you wouldn't make love to me here, in your—our—grandmother's house,' she reminded him.

'Does that mean you would be more responsive to me if I invited you to mine?' he demanded.

'*No!*' Harriet looked him in the eye and told the one lie that she knew would put an end to all this dangerous skirmishing. 'I'm in love with someone else.' At least, Rosa was.

The effect on Leo was instant. A feeling of desolation crept over Harriet as she watched the desire drain from his eyes, replaced by the coolness of their first meeting. 'So. You are unchanged after all. You still like to flirt with danger. If you had told me this at the start I would not have touched you!'

'I'm sorry,' she said miserably, then gave him a forlorn little smile. 'But you're here, Leo. It's only natural I still feel drawn towards you.'

Leo moved towards her, suddenly menacing in his cold anger. 'Dante is also your cousin. Did you allow *him* to kiss you?'

'No, of course not,' she said, appalled, but he gave a short, mirthless laugh.

'How do I know that's true?'

'You could always ask him,' she snapped, suddenly furious. 'Maybe you should ask Franco, too, make sure I didn't try to lure him away from Mirella! *You* haven't changed, either, Leo. You thought the worst of me all those years ago, and you still do.' She turned on her heel, but Leo caught her by the arm before she could open the door.

'Who is he?' he demanded.

Harriet looked at him blankly.

'This man you are in love with!' he said through his teeth.

'I'd rather not say,' she said with hauteur.

To her consternation Leo smiled, visibly relaxed. 'You mean you lied,' he said triumphantly. 'There is no secret lover.'

'Believe what you please,' she said, suddenly weary. 'I'm tired, Leo. I want to go to bed.'

He took her in his arms, holding her close with a tenderness which brought sudden tears to her eyes. Leo tipped her face back, then bent to kiss the tears away. 'You have done so much to make Nonna's birthday happy, and I am keeping you from your bed. Give me one kiss good-night, little cousin, and I shall let you go.'

Harriet held up her face obediently, then remembered the harm she could do Rosa, and pulled away. 'No, Leo. I can't.'

His face hardened into a cold, unforgiving mask. 'You mean you won't. But I refuse to believe this story about a mystery lover.'

'That's your privilege,' she returned.

'And perhaps you are wiser than I. You caused havoc with my life once. I would be mad to allow you to do it again.' Leo smiled with glacial politeness. 'I'm afraid Nonna's dream must go unrealized.'

Harriet frowned. 'What do you mean?'

'She told me this evening that she was so happy that you and I were friends again, and made it plain that she would like us to be more than that.' Leo raised a quizzical eyebrow. 'You had no idea of this?'

She shook her head violently. '*No*. No, I didn't. If I'd thought there was the slightest possibility of it I'd never have come.' And that, she thought miserably, was the simple truth.

Leo bowed formally. 'You make yourself very plain, Rosa. So plain that I will relieve you of my company for the remainder of your visit. Goodbye.' He turned on his heel and strode from the room.

Harriet removed her shoes and went to make sure the door was locked, then went slowly up the shallow stone stairs. She closed her bedroom door behind her and stripped off the clinging dress, went through the automatic motions of preparing for the night, and in bed at last reminded herself that Rosa had told her not to get friendly with Leo. So if he was angry with his 'cousin' nothing had changed.

Next morning Harriet was so tired it was an effort to discuss the party over breakfast.

'You should have sent Leo away earlier last night,' said Vittoria Fortinari indulgently.

'He didn't stay long, Nonna,' said Harriet, thinking how easy it was to think of Signora Fortinari as her own grandmother.

The signora, who was also looking decidedly weary

after the exertions of the previous evening, gave Harriet a loving smile. 'It does my heart so much good to see you and Leo friends again, my dearest. I know I am a foolish old woman, but I cannot help hoping that perhaps you and Leo might become more than friends one day, now that all is forgiven and forgotten.'

Harriet was about to say, once and for all on Rosa's behalf, this this was out of the question, when she saw the other woman change colour and catch her breath. 'What is it?' she asked urgently. 'Nonna—are you ill?'

Signora Fortinari sat back in her chair, breathing shallowly. 'My pills,' she said with difficulty. 'In my room—by the bed—'

Harriet yelled for Silvia as she tore upstairs, opened a wrong door before she found the right one, found the pills then raced down to the dining room, and knelt by Signora Fortinari's chair, chafing the cold hands.

'Shall I ring the doctor?' she said anxiously.

'No, child.' The voice was breathless but reassuringly firm. 'All I need is a little pill under the tongue and I shall be well.'

A few minutes later Vittoria Fortinari was installed on the sofa in the salon, with Harriet in a chair close beside her. The 'little pill' had begun to do its work, and her face had regained some colour.

'Feeling better?' asked Harriet.

'Much better. Silvia fusses so.' The other woman smiled ruefully. 'I was foolish to stay up so late. But I was enjoying my party. If I do not reach another birthday I shall be happy now.'

'Don't talk like that!' implored Harriet. 'You'll

have lots more birthdays.' And, God willing, Rosa would be here in future to share them.

The signora smiled lovingly. 'Dear child. How glad I am that you came. And how much I regret not sending for you sooner. Can you forgive me?'

'Please don't talk of forgiveness,' said Harriet, stricken with guilt. 'Let's just enjoy our time together before I leave.'

'Must you go home so soon, Rosa?' The shadowed dark eyes met Harriet's with entreaty. 'Can you not stay a little longer?'

'Not this time, Nonna.' Harriet smiled shakily. 'I have to get back to work. Tony needs me.'

'Of course.' Signora Fortinari sighed. 'I am a selfish old woman.' She smiled at Harriet ruefully. 'So selfish I must say what is in my heart. Last night it was obvious to me—and not only to me—that you and Leo care for each other. Otherwise I would stay silent. But because I believe you are in love with him, and he with you, now you have met again, it is my dearest wish to see you married to each other before I die.'

Harriet stared at her in helpless dismay. 'But Nonna,' she said hoarsely, then cleared her throat and tried again. 'It's really not a good idea. For one thing, we're first cousins—'

'This is not an insurmountable obstacle,' said the signora dismissively. Her keen eyes met Harriet's. 'Can you honestly tell me you care nothing for Leo?'

Defeated, Harriet shook her head slowly. 'Not that it makes any difference. Leo finds me attractive enough, I know, but—'

'You mean he desires you!'

Harriet smiled crookedly. 'Possibly. But that doesn't mean he wants to marry me.'

'I think it does. It is time Leo had a wife,' said the signora firmly, then patted Harriet's hand. 'Now I shall have a little sleep. So rest, Rosa, or sit on the loggia with a book.'

Harriet felt too restless to sit, or read, wanting nothing more than to run for home right that moment, before life became so complicated she would never again be able to unravel it. Once she was sure the signora was resting comfortably, Harriet told Silvia she was going out into the garden, and wandered off to explore the paths which led between formal flower beds and high hedges to concealed flights of shallow, mossy steps, one of which led to a small round pool where a stone cherub blew on a conch shell which spouted drops of glittering water. Harriet sat beside it for a while, wishing vainly for what might have been. Afterwards, still restless, Harriet went into the house to collect her bag and peep in on the sleeping invalid, then went out outside again to climb a steep slope to the terrace behind the villa, where a chestnut tree shaded the ruin of what had obviously once been some kind of chapel in the far distant past.

Inside the chapel's crumbling, ruined walls, glad of the shade from the chestnut tree, Harriet sat down on the ground and leaned back against the cold stone. She closed her eyes, feeling so tired suddenly that her mind refused to grapple with problems which seemed to be multiplying by the hour. With a sigh she took the cellphone from her bag and rang her mother briefly, then rang the number Rosa had given her for emergencies, only to be told that Miss Mostyn was away for the day.

No help in that direction then. Harriet put the phone away and tried to comfort herself with the thought that this time tomorrow she would be on her way home from Tuscany, and would never meet Signora Fortinari or Leo again. Instead of comforting her the thought made her so wretched she laid her head down on her knees and gave way to silent tears, unaware that she had company until she heard a hard, hostile voice.

'Revisiting the scene of your crime?'

Harriet tensed, then raised her head, knuckling away the tears as she stared up resentfully at Leo Fortinari. His face altered dramatically at the sight of her wet face and swollen eyes. He dropped to his knees beside her and took her hands.

'What is it, Rosa?' he demanded urgently. 'Are you ill?'

She shook her head. 'No. But Nonna was, after breakfast.'

'I know. Silvia rang me.'

'So that's why you're here,' she said thickly, and detached her hands to search in her bag for tissues.

'Partly,' said Leo, watching her mop herself up. 'Silvia told me Nonna tired herself too much last night and needed one of her heart pills, but it was nothing serious.'

'It seemed serious enough to me,' said Harriet with a shudder, and Leo put his arm round her, holding her close.

'I have just seen Nonna. She's fine. She sent me to look for you.'

'I didn't hear your car,' said Harriet unsteadily, knowing she should pull away. But after today she would never feel Leo's touch again, or hear his voice;

a thought which plunged her so deep into depression again she buried her wet face against Leo's shirt.

Leo sat back against the ruined wall, holding her close as he smoothed her hair, his breath warm against her ear as he murmured words of comfort she could only half understand in her present state of distress.

'This is the last place I thought to find you,' he said, when she was calmer. 'No wonder you are crying.'

Harriet tensed. Leo had said something about the scene of the crime. She looked up to find his eyes narrowed with sudden urgency.

'Now that we are here, tell the truth, Rosa. Did you send for me that day just to make sure I found you here with Guido?'

'I can't remember.' Harriet scrambled quickly to her feet, brushing dust from her jeans, her eyes refusing to meet his.

Leo stood up and leaned against the wall. When she remained silent his mouth twisted, and he turned to point at the space below what had once been an altar. 'Perhaps I should refresh your memory. Try to imagine how I felt when I heard you scream. I rushed up here to find you struggling, terrified, there on the ground beneath Guido Bracco. You were screaming at him to stop, but by the time I wrenched him away from you it was too late, the damage was done. I ordered you into the house then gave Guido a thrashing which relieved the fury I felt for both of you, but otherwise did more harm than good.'

Harriet hid her face in her hands in horror.

'I assume that you offered such temptation,' went on Leo sternly, 'that Guido forgot all the rules of his upbringing and religion just to have you.'

Harriet shuddered. 'Stop, Leo, *please!*'

'No, Rosa. You should know that Guido cried like a baby when I'd finished with him, and suffered such agonies of remorse he swore he would keep silent. Which he did. And everyone believed I was a monster to administer a beating over a few stolen kisses. But I had to tell Nonna the truth. And for once she was deaf to your pleading, and informed your parents. Which caused wounds it has taken years to heal. But now you have been reunited with her at last, and made her birthday happy. And for that I am grateful to you.' He moved closer. 'But you know that I feel more than just grateful to you, Rosa.'

Harriet stared past him, feeling queasy. 'I'm surprised you even want to touch me,' she said bitterly.

'You were very young. You made a mistake and you paid for it.' He took her hand. 'But not as much as you could have. It is a miracle there was no child.'

Harriet shuddered, then pulled herself together. 'Would you do something for me, Leo?'

'Of course.'

'Can you smuggle me into the house without Nonna seeing me like this?'

He nodded. 'Though I must warn you that she has invited me to lunch.'

Harriet decided on attack. 'In that case you ought to know that this morning she told me it's her dearest wish to see us married before she dies, Leo. To each other,' she added.

He smiled crookedly. 'I know. I think it was always her wish. That is why she was so angry with you over the episode with Guido.'

'I was no longer pure and perfect enough for Leonardo Fortinari!'

He shrugged. 'More or less. But you were a temptress from your cradle, Rosa. Looking back, I'm amazed I never gave in to you myself that summer.' He sobered. 'I wish now that I had. It would have saved a lot of trouble.'

How right he was, thought Harriet miserably, as she followed Leo down to the villa. He distracted Silvia's attention long enough for Harriet to get to her room, where she worked swiftly on her face and hair, her mind in turmoil. She now knew why Rosa had been unwilling to return here unmarried and pregnant. No wonder she'd kept the details to herself, either. Otherwise, thought Harriet, nothing would have persuaded her to come here. But she had come. And met Leo Fortinari. And there was just today to go before she could abandon this risky masquerade and run for home.

Harriet went downstairs to find Signora Fortinari so deep in conversation with Leo neither of them noticed her until she coughed to announce her presence.

Looking a little flustered, the signora beckoned her over to her sofa, and patted the place beside her. 'Come and sit here, dearest. Leo cannot stay to lunch after all.'

'What a shame.' Harriet shot a look at Leo's inscrutable face, wondering what they'd been discussing so gravely. 'How are you feeling, Nonna?' she asked.

'A little better.' Vittoria Fortinari smiled bravely. 'Forgive me for frightening you, dearest. This heart of mine is very tiresome. I can see you have been crying. I am so sorry to have upset you.'

'It was a bit of a shock,' admitted Harriet, and did her best to smile.

'Since I must go now, Rosa, I persuaded Nonna to spare you for dinner with me this evening,' said Leo.

Harriet stared at him, startled. 'But I'm leaving in the morning—'

'I know,' said the signora quickly. 'And though I desire every minute of your company, Rosa, I must retire to bed early after the excesses of last night. Silvia will be on hand to look after me, so Leo can ensure you enjoy your last evening here. Last for the time being,' she amended, smiling lovingly.

Leo got up quickly. 'I shall come for you at eight, Rosa.'

Whether she agreed or not. 'Then of course I shall be ready,' she said, resigned.

'See Leo out, Rosa,' said Signora Fortinari, 'and tell Silvia we are ready for lunch.'

Harriet delivered her message, then walked down the steps with Leo to his car. 'You don't have to entertain me this evening,' she said curtly. 'I would be quite happy in my room with a book after Nonna goes to bed.'

He raised a sardonic eyebrow. 'That is unflattering, Rosa. But if you wish I can ask Dante along, also Mirella and Franco, if you are afraid to dine alone with me.'

She gave him a long, slow look under lowered lashes, but refused to rise to his taunt.

He raised an eyebrow. 'Do you know what happens when you look at a man like that, Rosa?'

Since it was a mannerism discovered only that minute Harriet had no idea. 'Don't worry, Leo,' she said sweetly. 'You're in no danger from me.'

He let out an explosive breath then pulled her into his arms. 'You are mistaken,' he said against her mouth. 'Every moment we are together the danger increases.' He kissed her hard, then raced down to the car in a manner more characteristic of Dante than the lofty Leonardo Fortinari.

CHAPTER SIX

HARRIET WATCHED THE BLUE MASERATI out of sight until her pulse settled down, then went inside to join Signora Fortinari in the dining room.

'You will enjoy your evening much more with Leo, Rosa,' said the signora, her eyes taking in the flush on Harriet's cheeks. 'It makes me so happy to see you on friendly terms with him again.'

Which was a very understated way to describe the idiocy of being head over heels in love with a man she'd known for a mere two days, thought Harriet despairingly.

When Leo came for her, later that evening, Harriet kissed Rosa's grandmother good-night with a feeling of excitement mingled with dread. So far she'd spent only limited periods of time actually alone with Leo Fortinari. Tonight, on a one-to-one basis for an entire evening, enormous care would be necessary to keep up the imposture to the very last minute.

'You are very quiet,' commented Leo, as he eased the Maserati down the vertiginous bends to the main road. 'Are you worried about Nonna?'

'Yes,' said Harriet truthfully. 'How serious is her condition?'

Leo shot a sidelong glance at her. 'Her doctor is noncommittal. With care she might last for years, he says. But no more parties from now on. And stressful situations must be avoided at all costs.'

Like hassle from troublesome granddaughters,

thought Harriet, receiving his message loud and clear. 'A pity,' she commented quietly. 'Nonna enjoyed her party so much.'

'Something which your presence greatly enhanced, of course.'

'Thank you. I was glad to be there.' Which wasn't the unalloyed truth, but Harriet was sincerely glad nothing had marred Signora Fortinari's day. Even the wine-throwing episode with Sophia Rossi had merely amused the birthday girl. 'I expect you can guess the other reason for my lack of sparkle,' she went on quietly.

'You mean my lecture in the garden.' He put out a hand to touch hers. 'If I made you unhappy I am sorry, Rosa. But when I found you there, in that particular place, it seemed best to lay old ghosts.'

'I'm sure you're right. Where are you taking me?' she added, surprised as they bypassed the village. Signora Fortinari had told her the trattoria there was one of Leo's regular eating places.

'I thought you would like to see my house,' he said casually, startling her. 'Which is very different from the family home at Fortino. Though you rarely came there, for some reason.'

Because Rosa had apparently been very much in awe of Maria Fortinari, Leo's mother, and the renaissance-style villa overlooking the vineyards had been too formal and grand for the youthful visitor. Rosa had always stayed at the less palatial Villa Castiglione, the house Vittoria Fortinaro had inherited from her own family.

'I was afraid of your mother,' said Harriet, quoting Rosa. 'Your mother disapproved of me, I'm afraid. Though your father was always sweet to me.'

'As all men have been since your birth!'

'Except you.'

'I have changed,' he said softly, keeping his eyes on the road. 'So have you, Rosa.'

Wishing he wouldn't keep saying something that was so much more the truth than he knew, Harriet exclaimed with pleasure as the Fortino vineyards came into view. In the brilliant moonlight a tall bell tower drew the eye to a house big enough to be the 'palace' that had awed the young Rosa. Beyond it Harriet could see a cluster of buildings where the famous Fortinari wine was processed. 'I'd—forgotten how beautiful it is,' she said, then looked up at Leo, surprised, as he drove on past the group of buildings crowning the endless slopes of the vineyards. 'Where do *you* live then, Leo?'

'Only a kilometre or so away. Near enough for convenience, but far enough to feel I leave my labours behind at night. Some nights, at least.'

Leo Fortinari's house was architecturally very similar to the Villa Castiglione, but inside it was very different. Instead of painted ceilings, and gilding and ormolu, Leo's taste ran to plain dark wood and natural linen, with very few paintings on the stark white walls, and only an occasional rug on the gleaming wood floors.

Harriet liked it a lot, and said so very emphatically.

'You mean that?' said Leo, surprised. 'No one else does. According to my mother it looks like an art gallery.'

'I can see what she means,' conceded Harriet. 'It must be wonderfully cool in the heat of summer.' She turned to look at him. 'I like this uncluttered kind of comfort, but it comes as a surprise after the exterior.'

'It was almost a ruin when I acquired it, and needed much restoration. You are the first to show enthusiasm,' he added dryly. 'Most women yearn to add cushions and mirrors and flowers the minute they set foot inside.'

I bet they do, thought Harriet. She smiled at him. 'Then I'm glad to be the exception.'

'By "most women",' he said, looking down into her eyes, 'I mean Nonna, and my mother, also Mirella. The renovation has only recently been completed. No other woman outside the family has ever been here.'

'Then I'm honoured,' said Harriet, and turned away to look at a painting of the Fortino vineyards, a blurred, impressionist study of sunlight on golden buildings and endless, serried rows of vines. 'I love this. Did you commission it?'

'Yes,' said Leo, standing close behind her. 'Do you still draw, Rosa? Your sketchbook was always with you at one time.'

Full of drawings of a younger Leo Fortinari, as Harriet knew only too well. 'No,' she said flatly, just in case her own nonexistent artistic talent might be called on. 'I don't have time.'

'A pity,' he commented, and took her hand. 'Come and talk to me in the kitchen while I prepare the meal.'

Harriet eyed him in mock astonishment as they went into a very modern, functional kitchen so unlike his grandmother's the two rooms could have been on different planets. 'You can cook?'

He laughed. 'Is that so hard to believe?'

'Yes,' said Harriet candidly, eyeing the perfection of his ice-blue shirt and pale linen trousers.

Leo filled a large steel pan with water and set it on the stove to boil. He removed the cork from a bottle of wine, then invited Harriet to inspect the contents of a pan he took from a vast refrigerator. 'My mother's cook made this sauce for me this morning. I am to heat it gently, throw pasta into the boiling water, then toss a salad with oil and vinegar—and dinner will be ready.'

Harriet laughed. 'So that's what you mean by cooking!'

Leo grinned in response. 'Is there something else you'd prefer?'

'No. Nothing at all.' Which was the truth. She couldn't have cared less what she ate tonight as long as she shared the meal alone with Leo Fortinari. As a reward for the nervous strain of her visit, crowned by the revelations of the morning, she deserved this one evening before she left.

Leo had set the table in his dining room, which looked out over the moonlit vista of his family vineyards. 'We shall dine by candlelight,' he said, as he seated Harriet in a chair facing arched windows.

Feeling more than ever like Cinderella with the clock ticking fast towards midnight, Harriet set herself to relish every moment of Leo's company over the simple, perfect meal and the silk-smooth wine as they talked on a variety of subjects, and by unspoken consent avoided any mention of the past. For the first time since her arrival Harriet felt totally at ease in his company, but afterwards refused offers of pudding.

'Thank you, but I'll pass,' said Harriet with regret. 'I shouldn't have mopped my plate with this wonderful bread.'

'I will remember to give you less next time you

dine here,' said Leo, his eyes reflecting the flickering candlelight. 'How soon can you return, Rosa?'

'I don't know,' she said sadly.

'If your responsibilities were less pressing, would you stay?'

She drew in a deep breath, and smiled a little. 'Oh yes, Leo. I would. But for one reason and another that isn't possible.'

He nodded soberly. 'I understand the burden of responsibility very well.' He stood up, holding out his hand. 'Come back to the kitchen while I make coffee.'

Harriet smiled wryly. 'I'd prefer to pass on the coffee, too. Otherwise I'll never sleep tonight.'

His smile sent a tremor through her. 'Lately, sleeping is difficult for me, also.' He took her hand in his, and kept it there until they were sitting together on one of his sofas. He half turned to face her, and Harriet tensed as she met the look in his eyes. 'It has been a great pleasure,' he said with emphasis, 'just to be with you and dine with you tonight, but this was not the sole reason for asking you to spend time with me.'

Harriet sat motionless, her eyes locked with his. Was this it, at last? she thought in alarm, her heart thudding under the gossamer wool of Rosa's dress. Perhaps the meal and the conversation that had flowed so easily had merely been some kind of overture to the unmasking ceremony she had dreaded every minute since her arrival.

'Why then?' she said, her mouth so parched the words came out in a whisper.

'You know that I desire you,' he said huskily. 'You are so different now you are a woman, little cousin, that I would be happy to agree to Nonna's request to make *her* happy before she dies.'

Harriet passed the tip of her tongue round dry lips, as Leo went on to say that his grandmother wished them to marry.

'She is old and frail, and is stricken by remorse for her estrangement from you all these years. Also she blames me for my part in this. Now, she says, I have the opportunity to make up for this and bring you back into the fold. So, will you consent to an engagement, if nothing else?' His eyes sent a frisson of apprehension down her spine. 'Nonna is unlikely to remain with us very long. If the thought of marriage daunts you this might never be necessary. But you could make her very happy while she lives.' He took her hands in his, and Harriet stared down at them in utter misery.

'You've forgotten—' she started hoarsely, then cleared her throat and began again. 'There's someone else in my life, Leo.'

'I refuse to believe that he is important to you,' he said arrogantly, and pulled her into his arms. 'Otherwise, you would not tremble at my touch,' he whispered, gazing deep into her eyes. 'Can you deny that you respond to me?'

'That's not the point,' said Harriet desperately, and tried to pull away, but he laughed softly, and pulled her closer.

'If you prefer we could just pretend to be engaged, just to give Nonna pleasure. You could continue with your work at the hotel for a while, if you insist—'

'Wouldn't that rather defeat the object?'

'No. You would return here every other week or so, of course, and I could come to visit you, as any fiancé with blood in his veins would insist.' Leo smiled at her indulgently. 'Is it so much to ask?'

Harriet nodded vigorously. 'Nonna would expect us to marry—'

'Has this lover of yours mentioned marriage?'

'That's not the point, Leo,' she retorted. 'You can't marry someone just to please your grandmother.'

He bent his head and kissed her hungrily. 'It would please *me*, also, believe me. And,' he added, his voice deepening to a note which played havoc with Harriet's defences, 'I will take great pleasure in demonstrating how much it will please *you*.'

He kissed her again, long, slow, vanquishing kisses that deprived her of all will to resist. She could feel his heart thudding in unison with her own, and suddenly Leo Fortinari stood up, pulling her with him, and before Harriet realised what he had in mind he picked her up and strode out of the room to the stairs leading from the shadowy hall to the upper floor.

'Leo, no,' she panted, struggling in his arms, but he laughed softly, and held her tightly. He mounted the stairs with a speed which left him panting when he collapsed with her on a bed in a large, moonlit room, pinning her down with the weight of his body.

'Nonna,' he said breathlessly, 'told me to use every power of persuasion in my command—'

'She can't have meant this!' Harriet reared up to free herself, but Leo pushed her down gently, silencing her with caresses which quickly aroused her to such a frenzied pitch of longing her will to resist dissolved. Yet in some small, still-functioning part of her mind she recognised that Leo's assault on her senses was deliberate. His eyes held hers relentlessly as he caressed and cajoled her body into quivering response, and now that it was too late she realised that every move he'd made during the evening had been carefully planned. The food, the wine, the easy conversation had been nothing more than skilled foreplay. And at last Harriet saw his eyes glaze with a frighteningly blind, molten sheen that told her Leo Fortinari no longer cared why he'd brought her here. His importuning hands and relentless mouth took on a new urgency, setting her entire body on fire in response to the kind of lovemaking she'd never experienced in her life.

Leo made verbal love to her with a stream of hot, liquid Italian her brain could no longer translate as he undressed her with urgent hands. Harriet let out a stifled groan as he kissed her breasts and caught a hard, proud nipple in his mouth, his teeth tugging with such consummate skill she felt as though he were drawing her soul from her body. The time for objections, she recognized in renewed panic, was long past, as his erect, naked body came into full contact with her own.

'Leo, no!' she said in sudden, violent desperation and tried to break free, 'You don't realise—I can't— you mustn't—'

'Ah, but you can, and I *must*,' he said hoarsely, and lifted her against him, so that she felt his arousal hard and quivering against her hot skin. 'This is what we were created for!'

Harriet gasped as his thrusting body joined with hers, causing such exquisite pain she clenched her teeth against the bittersweet anguish. Leo tensed for an instant, his eyes staring incredulously into hers, then he groaned, unable to control the powerful body which surged into urgent, unstoppable rhythm which transmuted the pain into sensation which soon became so ravishing Harriet had no defences left against the rapture of it.

But experienced lover though he was, it was over too soon for her, leaving her with the feeling that something wonderful had just eluded her as Leo gasped in the throes of fulfilment she longed to share.

Still breathing hard, Leo got up and stood at the edge of the bed, staring down at her, utterly oblivious of his nudity. Harriet scrambled up in sudden burning embarrassment, desperate to find her clothes, then realised what he was looking at, and flushed to the roots of her hair at the sight of bloodstains on the pristine cover.

Grim-faced, Leo tossed a towelling robe to her, and without a word went into the adjoining bathroom. He returned with a bath towel knotted round his lean hips, and stood over her like a judge passing sentence on a convicted criminal.

'So I was right. You are not Rosa. Who in God's name are you?' he demanded harshly.

CHAPTER SEVEN

HARRIET BELTED LEO FORTINARI'S robe tightly, refusing to meet his eyes as she faced the sheer stupidity of what she'd allowed to happen. What in heaven's name had she been thinking of? Which was the point, of course. After a while thinking hadn't come into it. For the first time in her entire life her mind had been defeated by the clamouring of her body. But recriminations were futile. To echo something Leo had said earlier, the damage was done.

'Before I answer that,' she said formally. 'May I use your bathroom?'

'Be quick then.' Leo collected his clothes then strode to the door. He turned, giving her a peremptory glare. 'I demand a full explanation. Come down when you are ready.'

It was obvious that Leo was in a towering rage. As well he might be, Harriet thought bleakly, as she turned on the shower. She wrapped her hair in a towel and stood under water as hot as she could bear, then ran it cold, and emerged shivering, to dress in the clothes Leo had strewn all over the bedroom floor. What a fool, she thought bitterly. After surviving a whole weekend without discovery, she'd lost her head completely and given Leo proof of the one blindingly obvious difference between herself and Rosa Mostyn.

When she went downstairs she found Leo in the kitchen. He gave her a brooding, hostile look, then put a coffee pot on the table, and motioned her to a chair, facing him.

In silence Harriet sat down, filled two cups, added sugar to his and passed it to him.

'You learn quickly,' he said, his face set in harsh lines. 'So tell me, Princess Incognita. Who are you? *What* are you? And,' he added, in a tone which made her quake, 'who paid you to deceive my grandmother?'

Harriet winced. 'I think you already know that.' She stirred sugar into her coffee, then looked up to meet his hard, demanding eyes.

'You mean Rosa!' he said in disgust. 'So there is no change after all. She is still up to her tricks.'

'You're wrong, Rosa *has* changed,' Harriet contradicted. 'She wanted quite desperately to come herself. She longs to be reunited with her grandmother, so please don't be too hard on her.'

'Hard on her? If she were here I would be more than just hard on her—' He frowned, his mouth twisting in distaste. 'This is ludicrous. How can we sit here and discuss the situation calmly when only a few minutes ago we were together in the most intimate situation a man and woman can share!'

She gulped down some of her coffee. 'I should have fought harder.'

His eyes narrowed malevolently between the thick lashes. 'Why didn't you?' His mouth twisted. 'As if I need to be told!'

Harriet looked blank. 'What do you mean?'

'Do you take me for a fool?' He drained his cup and set it down with a crash. 'You are not Rosa. Yet you allow me to be your first lover!' His smile turned her cold. 'It is obvious that you like the life here very much. Perhaps it is a great deal more pleasant than your own. However, if you think you can trap Leonardo Fortinari by the oldest trick known to woman, you are mistaken.'

Harriet felt stunned for a moment, then anger flared hotly to meet his own. 'I expected a meal in some restaurant, not here. And I certainly didn't expect a session in bed to pay for my supper, Signor Fortinari.' She glared at him. 'I tried to put a stop to things, if you remember, but you wouldn't listen to me. You're a lot bigger and stronger than me, and because I've never been in the same situation before I had no idea—' She stopped abruptly, and looked away, breathing in deeply to gain control of her temper.

'No idea of what?' he demanded.

'That eventually I wouldn't be able to prevent what happened.' She lifted her head to meet his eyes. 'Don't be frightened—'

'*Frightened?*' he shot at her.

'Frightened about my intentions.' She smiled at him kindly. 'Don't worry, *Signor* Fortinari. No one will know about tonight from me. It's not something I'm proud of, believe me.' She frowned thughtfully. 'But I'll be honest and admit that after a while it wasn't only you I was fighting but myself. You must be a skilled lover, I should think.'

'You should *think?*' He glared at her, incensed.

Harriet glared back. 'Comparisons aren't possible, are they?'

He snarled something under his breath, then sat back in his chair, making a visible effort to control his anger. Harriet waited, determined not to explain until he asked again, and at last he leaned forward, his eyes boring into hers. 'So. Tell me who you are.

How are you involved with my cousin? Are you an actress?'

She shook her head. 'My name is Harriet Foster, I once went to the same school as Rosa, and I'm a schoolteacher.'

Leo stared at her blankly. 'With such a resemblance surely you must be related in some way to Rosa?'

'No,' she said, resigned. 'It's just a freak of nature. When we were younger Rosa and I really hated the resemblance.'

Leo leaned back in his chair again, his eyes hooded as they studied her face. 'Which is a very remarkable one, Miss Foster.'

She smiled involuntarily at the formality, winning an angry look from Leo.

'You find the situation amusing?' he cut at her. 'I do not.'

'Not amusing, Mr. Fortinari,' she said deliberately. 'But under the circumstances the formality struck me as oddly irrelevant.'

He relaxed slightly. 'I owe you an apology,' he said stiffly. 'I should not have made love to you.' His eyes locked with hers. 'But from the moment you arrived I had doubts. You looked like Rosa, yet there was a subtle difference. From the first I was drawn to you in a way I had never felt for my cousin. But I persuaded myself that the years since our last meeting, also the recent tragedy, were responsible for the changes in you. I told myself that to make love to you would provide the answer. If you were not Rosa you would naturally not allow it. If you were—' He shrugged. 'Then you had changed enough to make it easy for me to agree to Nonna's plan.'

'To get together just to please Signora Fortinari,' she said resigned. 'Only I'm not Rosa after all. I'm sorry. I had no idea you were bringing me here tonight. I suppose I should have demanded to go back to the Villa the moment we arrived. If I had I might have carried out the deception until I left. Then no one would have been hurt, or any the wiser.'

'But I told you that Rosa lost her virginity to Guido Bracco on the day I recalled in such detail to you.' Leo's mouth twisted. 'Did you think I wouldn't *notice?*'

Harriet looked him in the eye. 'Thinking didn't come into it. For which your expertise is partly to blame.'

'I blame myself for all of it,' he retorted bitterly. 'I must have been mad. I have no excuse. I drank only a glass or so of wine. But it felt so good just to be with you, to talk and share a meal together. There was such rapport between us I *wanted* you to be Rosa.' Leo eyed her as though he still couldn't believe it, then threw out his hands. 'You felt as though you belonged in my arms. By the time I found I was making love to a virgin it was too late. My body was programmed for the ecstasy I experienced in your arms.' His mouth twisted. 'For the first time I am able to understand why Guido Bracco behaved as he did with Rosa. Once I began to make love to you, Harriet Foster, I could not have stopped if the house had come crashing down about our ears.'

Harriet stared at him mutely, feeling heat flood her entire body.

'Tell me just one thing before we discuss the hard facts of the situation, Miss Foster,' said Leo after a while. 'Did you derive any pleasure from our encounter? Or did I hurt you too much?'

'Are you asking for marks for your performance?' she asked acidly, and had the satisfaction of seeing colour rise in his lean face.

'No, I am not,' he retorted, teeth clenched. He took in a deep breath. 'But I would regret causing such pain and disgust you will never wish to repeat the experience.'

'With you?' she queried sweetly, feeling oddly liberated now she could be herself instead of constantly trying to curry favour for Rosa. 'Not a chance, Signor Fortinari.'

Leo sat back in his chair, his eyes oddly blank. 'I suppose,' he said slowly, 'I meant with other men in future.'

'Other men,' she repeated thoughtfully.

'One man, then,' he snapped. 'You must have someone back in England. Unless all your men friends are eunuchs?'

'No. Normal to a man, every last one of them. If anyone's lacking in that way it's me,' she said with regret, because now it was blazingly obvious that the only thing lacking in her life had been Leo Fortinari, the one man in the world, it seemed, able to set her alight.

He raised a taunting eyebrow. 'You mean you preferred your own sex?'

'As it happens, no,' she retorted. 'Not that my sexual preferences are any of your business.'

Leo smiled wryly. 'You are right. I appologize, Rosa.'

'Harriet,' she corrected.

'Harriet,' he repeated, as though the truth was still

hard to swallow. 'It is time you told me how, and why, Rosa persuaded you to impersonate her.'

'I can tell you how, Leo, but I can't tell you why. That's for Rosa to do.'

'And when is she likely to do that?'

'I've no idea.'

Leo frowned. 'Does Tony know about this?'

'Heavens no.' Harriet shivered a little. 'Just Rosa, my mother, and myself. And now you.'

'Did she pay you well?' he demanded.

Harriet flushed. 'In a way.' Reluctantly, she gave the pressing reasons for her agreement to Rosa's plan. 'All Rosa wanted in exchange for the necessary funds was for me to take her place this weekend. Because, as must be obvious, I'm the only person in the world equipped to do it. I studied in Siena as a student, which is why I speak Italian well enough for the switch.' She met his eyes in sudden appeal. 'In the beginning, Leo, I said no very emphatically. Please believe that. But Rosa's so fond of my mother she grew very emotional about her health—understandably, because she's still grieving for her own mother. In the end Rosa made it impossible for me to refuse.'

'And how did she manage that?' he asked coolly.

'By her determination to pay for my mother's operation whether I came to Italy or not.'

'And your pride wouldn't allow that?'

'Exactly.'

'But you still can't tell me why Rosa couldn't come herself,' he said curtly.

'No. Sorry. I'm sure Rosa will tell Nonna soon—I mean your grandmother,' she amended awkwardly.

'I can tell you find it very easy to think of her as

your own.' Leo's anger diminished visibly. 'Does Nonna resemble your own grandmother?'

'No. Not in the least.'

'Then either you are a consummate actress, or you took to Nonna on sight.'

Harriet nodded. 'I was horribly nervous beforehand, but the moment I met her I felt as though I'd known her all my life.' Her eyes fell. 'To be honest, Leo, she feels far more like my grandmother than my own ever did.'

'The feeling is mutual. Nonna is very fond of you,' Leo conceded.

'But she thinks I'm Rosa.'

'And we shall let her go on thinking that,' he said with decision. 'There is no point in upsetting her needlessly.'

'No,' said Harriet unhappily. 'I suppose there isn't. But please believe one thing, Leo. I hated deceiving her.'

'Did you hate deceiving me?'

'Of course I did,' she said, her eyes falling.

'But now *I* am deceived no longer.' He stared at her broodingly. 'I have known you for such a short time, I discover, yet it feels like a lifetime. I think it will be a long, long time before I forget you, Harriet Foster.'

Ditto, thought Harriet bitterly. 'Will you drive me back now, please?'

Leo rose to his feet. 'There is something we must discuss first. I shall drive you to the airport tomorrow, but this must be settled tonight.'

'What do you mean?' she asked.

'The problem of a child that may be born from this night,' he said bluntly, taking Harriet's breath away.

She jumped up, hugging her arms across her chest in utter dismay. 'I hadn't thought of it—' She stopped short, then gave him a bitter little smile. 'Oh, I see. That's what you meant by traps, of course. Have no fear, Signor Fortinari. I wouldn't take a penny from you. Nor would I want you to marry me. Marriage is the last thing I want. Even with the great Leonardo Fortinari himself.'

Leo's mouth tightened, the hostile silence following her words lengthening unbearably. 'Nevertheless,' he snapped at last, 'you will keep me informed.'

Though she couldn't imagine doing so, no matter what happened, Harriet acquiesced, too tired for argument as Leo took a slim wallet from his back pocket and took out a card.

'This has both my numbers. You could reach me at the vineyard at any time, but for privacy it is better to ring here. Tell me,' he added suddenly. 'I own to feeling curious, Harriet. Why has no man ever tried to make love to you before this?'

She shrugged. 'Some have tried, but I never felt the slightest response. My lack of enthusiasm has been quite a drawback to lasting relationships. One thing I might say in your favour, Leo,' she added honestly, 'you made my first experience of—'

'Love?'

'Is that what it was?'

'How else would you describe it?' he asked, moving nearer.

'I don't know. Whatever it was I had no idea it would be like that.'

'Like what?'

She thought for a moment. 'So overwhelming.'

Leo frowned. 'Harriet, how old are you?' he demanded.

'Twenty-six.'

'And yet by your own choice you have never made love.' To her surprise he took her hand and kissed it. 'Forgive me, Harriet. Tonight I gave you no choice at all.'

'I'm partly to blame,' she said with justice, and detached her hand. 'I should have made you listen.'

'I am fortunate you are capable of such dispassionate reasoning! You have Rosa's face, but the personality behind it is very much your own, Harriet Foster.' He smiled derisively. 'No wonder I found Rosa so changed.'

'You thought you were making love to Rosa,' she pointed out.

Leo shook his head. 'I was making love to the woman I believed Rosa had become. In other words, you, Harriet.' His eyes locked with hers. 'I have a disturbing feeling that I will regret this night for many nights to come.'

CHAPTER EIGHT

HARRIET SPENT A RESTLESS, tossing, sleepless night,
her only comfort the fact that she was leaving early
next morning. The goodbyes with Signora Fortinari
were harrowing, but the journey to the airport with
Leo was even harder to bear.

'How do you feel this morning?' he asked curtly,
once they were on their way to Pisa.

'Tired.'

'You slept badly?'

'Yes.'

'So did I.'

There was silence for a while, then Harriet told him
how terrible she'd felt when it came to parting with
his grandmother. 'I almost blurted the truth.'

'It is good you did not,' he said forcefully. 'Time
enough for her to learn the facts when Rosa consents
to clear up the mystery. I was tempted to fly back
with you and confront her myself—'

'No!' said Harriet in alarm. 'Let her do things in
her own way. Please, Leo.'

He sent a brooding look at her pale, weary face.
'Very well.'

They said very little more until they were at the
airport.

'Don't wait,' pleaded Harriet, but Leo was obdu-
rate.

'I shall stay until the plane leaves.'

They sat together in tense, uncomfortable silence

for the mercifully short wait, oblivious of the crowds milling about them, and the incessant information coming over the sound system.

'Ring me as soon as you get home,' commanded Leo at one point.

'I shall ring Nonna—I mean—'

'I know! But ring my house afterwards. I shall be waiting.'

Harriet's eyes fell before the look in his, and she stared down at her clasped hands, deeply thankful that the flight to Heathrow was due to leave on time. It was a uniquely agonizing pleasure to sit close to Leo like this, knowing that these last few minutes were all they were ever likely to have together.

'You were so meek last night in promising to tell me about the child that it occurs to me you have no intention of doing so,' he said suddenly in her ear, and Harriet flinched. 'I demand that you will!'

When the flight was called they stood up, Harriet's face colourless as Leo stared down at her.

'Goodbye, Harriet Foster.'

'Goodbye.' She blinked hard to keep back the tears, and with a muttered exclamation he pulled her into his arms and kissed her with a prolonged, savage tenderness he very plainly intended to remain with her long after she'd boarded the plane.

In this, Leo Fortinari was successful. Fastened into her window seat Harriet stared, dazed, through the window, unaware of the man who sat next to her, and completely free of her usual nerves as the plane's engines roared into life for the take-off. At some point she unbuckled her seat-belt, and asked for tea in preference to the tray of food offered. But most of the flight went by in a blur as Harriet relived every mo-

ment in Leo's arms over and over again, touching a
finger to the lips which still throbbed from his kiss.

'Are you all right?' said her fellow passenger at
one point. 'Are you afraid of flying?'

Harriet gazed at the man blankly, then forced a
smile. 'No, not at all. Thank you.' She'd left her heart
back there in Tuscany, with someone who had no use
for it, but otherwise she was absolutely fine.

At Heathrow, while she waited for the coach that
would take her to Pennington, Harriet rang her mother
to say she'd landed. But to her consternation Rosa
answered.

'Harriet, thank God,' she said breathlessly.
'Claire's had to rush off to the hospital—'

'*What?* Why?' asked Harriet frantically. 'Did she
get worse suddenly—?'

'No, no, it's your *grandmother* who's ill, I came
round to visit Claire this morning, and arrived just in
time to call an ambulance. I followed them to the
hospital in case I could do anything, but Claire
wanted me to come back here to wait for you. I've
got so much to tell you. How did it go? Are you all
right?'

'Yes. Fine—I must dash, Rosa. The coach is load-
ing.'

'I'll meet you at the bus station.'

Enid Morris had been in and out of hospital for
years, and as the coach sped along the motorway
Harriet was beset by familiar guilt, as usual, because
she felt far more anxiety for her mother than the invalid. But Harriet's main preoccupation was the parting from Leo. No matter how much she told herself
it was silly to feel like this over a man she'd only
met four days ago life loomed bleak without him. She

gritted her teeth. If she'd been the kind to flit from one boyfriend's bed to another she might not have fallen so hopelessly in love. But if she had been a bed-hopper Leo would have been none the wiser anyway. Without the damning evidence that proved otherwise, to him she would still be his flighty little cousin. Instead he would probably always think of her as an opportunist who'd seized on a golden opportunity to profit from her association with Leo Fortinari.

When she saw Rosa waving energetically as the coach drew in Harriet smiled for the first time in hours. In tailored trousers and a fleece jacket Rosa's pregnancy was still undetectable. But something about her face was different, something visible to Harriet before she'd even left the coach. A new radiance shone in the huge dark eyes as Rosa hugged and kissed her as though they hadn't seen each other for months. Harriet, still unused to this new, affectionate Rosa, was taken aback at first, until she realised Rosa had company.

A slim, fair man, wearing dark glasses, stared at Harriet in amazement as he took her suitcase.

'This is Pascal,' said Rosa joyfully, and tried to take Harriet's flight bag, but Pascal forestalled her.

'No, *cherie*, you must be careful,' he scolded.

'Monsieur Tavernier, I presume,' said Harriet with a wry smile he returned in kind, his eyes incredulous behind the dark lenses.

'*Enchanté*. You can only be Miss Foster, of course. Rosa told me about the resemblance, but I did not believe her. It is extraordinary. May I call you Harriet?'

'Indeed you may. I'm so *very* glad to meet you!'

said Harriet, with an explosive sigh, then hugged Rosa close, glad that one of them, at least, found the future rosy.

With Pascal at the wheel of the Alfa Romeo, a highly excited Rosa sat in the back with Harriet, promising to go into detail later about the accident that had put Pascal out of action. The weekend had apparently been action-packed from the moment Harriet left. Allegra Mostyn had given birth to a son in the early hours of Saturday morning, and in the evening Rosa had heard from Pascal. Fizzing with excitement and joy, she demanded news of her grandmother, and everything that had happened, and Harriet duly reported on Signora Fortinari, and the party, and her own success in getting through the weekend without mishap, then asked to be set down at the hospital.

'Perhaps you wouldn't mind dropping the luggage off at our place on your way back, I'll hand your belongings over some other time.'

'Of course,' declared Rosa. 'We're not going anywhere yet. If it's all right with you I'll wait at your house with Pascal until you get back. I want more details from you.'

'But I might be a long time—'

'No matter.' Rosa smiled incandescently. 'We'll have more privacy at your place than at the Hermitage.' As they arrived at Pennington General Rosa laid a restraining hand on Harriet's. 'Just a minute. You haven't said a word about Leo. How did you get on with him?'

Harriet gave her a very wry little smile. 'Better than expected— but I'll tell you about it later. I'll hang on to your phone to ring Fortino, if you don't mind.'

'Of course not—but when you come home I want every last detail,' said Rosa, and got in the front with Pascal. 'We'll shop on the way back and get something in for a celebration meal.'

'Which I will cook,' said Pascal dryly. 'I hope you find your grandmother better, Harriet.'

Rosa nodded quickly. 'Me too. Give my love to Claire.'

Harriet waved them off, then rang the Villa Castiglione, a lump in her throat as she heard the anxiety in Signora Fortinari's voice.

'I am so glad to hear your voice, child. Now I can relax. Shall I give a message to Leo?' she added mischievously.

'He asked me to ring him after I'd spoken to you,' said Harriet quickly, knowing perfectly well the signora would read more into this than the facts.

When she rang Leo afterwards he answered immediately.

'Harriet,' she announced tersely.

'Are you at home?'

'No, at the hospital—'

'*Hospital?* Why? Are you ill?'

'No, not me, my grandmother.'

'Ah. I'm so sorry. What is wrong?'

'I don't know, I haven't seen her yet. I've just arrived. I rang Nonna first, but I must go now.'

'No, Harriet, wait,' he said urgently. 'You forgot to give me your number.'

'I didn't forget. It was deliberate.'

'But I must know—'

'No, Leo. I'll report to you. If necessary.' Not that she would.

'I don't want a *report*, Harriet. I want to talk to

you, make sure all is well.' He paused. 'I have had time to recover from my anger. To acknowledge that it is you who should be angry with me.'

'Oh I am,' she assured him. 'But I'm even angrier with myself. Just forget me, Leo. One Rosa at a time is enough for any family.'

'I don't want Rosa,' he said savagely. 'God help me, I want *you.*'

Harriet rang off, swallowing hard. She scrubbed at her damp eyes, then hurried to the inquiry desk for directions, and eventually found Claire Foster sitting slumped on a chair in a waiting room. She jumped up, her swollen eyes lighting up at the sight of her daughter.

Harriet flew to enfold her tall mother in her arms. 'How's Grandma?'

'Oh darling, I'm so glad to see you. Mother died a short time ago,' sobbed Claire, and buried her silver-streaked chestnut head on her daughter's shoulder. 'She complained of chest pains this morning, so they admitted her. Half an hour ago she suffered a massive heart attack and they couldn't revive her.'

'Oh *Mother,*' said Harriet, and hugged her close in remorse. 'I'm so sorry. I should have been here.'

'Rosa was a great help, despite her euphoria. You've met Pascal?' Claire managed a watery smile as she dried her eyes. 'They followed the ambulance here, but I sent them back to wait for your call.'

It was late afternoon before Harriet finally took her mother home to a sympathetic welcome from Rosa and Pascal. Afterwards the four of them spent a strange evening of sorrow, jubilation, curiosity and celebration all mixed together in a potent cocktail of emotions. During dinner Harriet described the weekend and the tightrope she'd walked so successfully, emphasizing Signora Fortinari's pleasure in the party, and laughing over the wine-spilling incident. But she took care to avoid too much mention of Leo. And after dinner Claire, utterly exhausted by that stage, gave in with very little argument when Harriet and Rosa persuaded her to go to bed.

'I'll come and see if you need anything later,' promised Harriet, kissing her mother good-night. 'But I'm not letting Pascal out of the house until I hear all about his adventures in the desert.'

Pascal was only too eager to explain that fate, not choice, had kept him away from Rosa. Tired and hot after covering a meeting between high-ranking French politicians and certain Arab leaders in Qatar, he had taken time off to visit a deserted beach for a swim, slept too long afterwards, and woke to find it was dark.

He'd set off at once to return to Doha, but missed the road in the darkness, and found himself stuck in soft sand, unable to move the car. His phone had run out of power, and he had no alternative but to stay where he was until sunrise. In the morning, motivated by raging thirst, he set out on foot to get help, but remembered nothing more until he woke in a strange room and learned that his elderly Arab host had found him unconscious by the roadside and taken him home to a village of cube-shaped houses clustered round a minaret.

'Heavens, you were lucky,' said Harriet in awe.

'I know it,' said Pascal, and pulled a shivering Rosa close. 'At first I could remember nothing, but at last my memory began to filter back, and the rest is history.' He shrugged expressively. 'As you say, Harriet, I am *very* lucky.'

'So am I,' said Rosa soberly, then gave Harriet a jubilant smile. 'You must be wondering what happens next. First on the agenda I shall write a long letter to Nonna to explain; you, Pascal, the baby, everything— and to soften the blow I shall enclose a wedding invitation.' She exchanged a tender look with Pascal. 'We're getting married in two weeks, Harriet, and we want you and Claire to be there.'

Harriet smiled in delight. 'How wonderful—congratulations!'

Pascal thanked her gracefully, but Rosa gave her a wicked grin. 'I warn you I'll have to invite Leo, too!'

Harriet's smiled vanished. 'In that case there's something you ought to know.' She gave Rosa a questioning look.

Rosa nodded in swift understanding. 'Talk away, Harriet. Pascal knows all my past sins.'

Harriet reluctantly confessed that Leo had given her all the details of the episode with Guido Bracco, and the trouble it had caused, both between Signora Fortinari and Huw Mostyn, and ultimately with Leo's own marriage prospects.

'Though I expect you know about that. And in the end I'm afraid I slipped up somewhere,' said Harriet, flushing. 'Leo found me out at the very last. Sorry, Rosa.'

Now Pascal was back Rosa didn't care in the slightest. 'I'm the one who should be apologizing, Harriet,' she said penitently. 'But I knew you wouldn't go if I told you everything. Leo was always going to be the main problem. Not that it matters, now, because I'll make full confession in my letter to

Nonna.' Rosa shivered, and Pascal's arm tightened round her protectively as she described the anguish of that long-ago wait to know if Guido had made her pregnant. 'But I never knew that his sister broke the engagement over it, Harriet, I swear. Was Leo utterly horrible to you?'

'Not really. Just—surprised.' Which was a ludicrously tame way to describe Leo's reaction when he discovered he'd made love to a stranger.

During the time before Enid Morris's funeral Harriet took leave from her job and Rosa spent every minute she could spare in the Foster household, helping with the funeral arrangements with the efficiency she brought to overseeing the Hermitage.

'What's going to happen about the hotel when you marry Pascal?' asked Harriet, over supper one evening.

'Tony's getting a new management team in. My hotel days are over. Anyway,' added Rosa, her eyes sparkling, 'Pascal's got a promotion. Instead of rushing round the world he'll be based in Paris from now on, which means I'm going to live there too, of course.' Her face sobered. 'I'm never letting him out of my sight again if I can possibly help it.'

'Don't smother him, love—let him breathe!' Claire smiled ruefully as she got up from the table. 'Sorry I'm such poor company at the moment, but I think I'll go up to bed. Don't go, Rosa. Stay and talk to Harriet for a while.'

Rosa was only too glad to. 'I couldn't tell you in front of your mother,' she said quickly, once Claire had left them, 'because I don't know exactly how much she knows, but Leo rang me at the Hermitage today, demanding your telephone number. No "congratulations on your wedding", or even "how is Tony's new son?" Just "give me Harriet's number".'

Harriet stared at her in dismay. 'And did you?'

'No way.' Rosa grimaced. 'He hasn't changed much, bossy as ever. Cousin Leo was in quite a strop when I said I had to ask you first.' Then she smiled. 'But when Nonna rang me it was a very different conversation, as you can imagine. Unlike Leo she was so loving and forgiving, and full of questions about you. Says she finds it all hard to take in.'

'Don't we all,' said Harriet, sighing. 'Can I tell Mother?'

'Of course. I didn't bang on about it while she was here.' Rosa sobered. 'Once the funeral is over I'll chat about it all as much as she likes, of course, when she's feeling better. Thank goodness the consultant can see her next week, Harriet.'

Harriet nodded fervently. 'Thank you for arranging the appointment so quickly, Rosa.'

'Don't thank me,' said Rosa, flushing. 'I'm the one in *your* debt. I feel guilty because there isn't a cloud in my sky. While you've got all this on your plate. In fact, Harriet, you look quite terrible. Are you all right?'

'I'm fine. Just a bit tired, that's all.'

Rosa looked unconvinced. 'So give me instructions. Do I give Leo your number?'

Harriet shook her head. 'I don't think so.'

The following evening Rosa was tied up with a big dinner at the Hermitage and for the first time since she was home Harriet ate supper alone with her mother.

'While you watch that play on television,' said

Harriet after she'd cleared away, 'I'll have a chat with Kitty.'

Claire smiled. 'Fine. Give her my love. Tell her to be here early tomorrow.'

'Will do,' said Harriet, and went upstairs to ring her sister. Afterwards, feeling tense and oddly guilty, she rang Leo's house.

'Pronto,' answered the familiar voice, its timbre reaching across the miles to send a shiver down to Harriet's toes.

'Leo, this is Harriet,' she said in English.

'Harriet! At last.'

So he could speak English. Harriet relaxed slightly.

'Rosa said you rang,' she went on.

'She refused to give me your number,' he said angrily. 'I demand that you give it to me at once, Harriet.'

'It's all right,' she assured him. 'You don't need it.'

'Cosa?' he said in disbelief. 'No need? Of course I need it!'

'I mean,' she said quickly, 'that there's no problem arising from our—our time together.'

'You mean you are not pregnant,' he said harshly.

'Yes. I mean, no, I'm not.'

'How long have you known?'

'Since yesterday.'

'And you are pleased?'

'Of course I'm pleased. I'm ecstatic,' she assured him. 'How is your grandmother?'

'She sends you warm greetings, and asks me to convey her condolences to you. I apologize, Harriet. I should have expressed my sympathy immediately.'

'Thank you.'

'How is your mother?'

'Very tired.'

'And how are you, Harriet?' he asked, his voice deepening. It sounded different in English, she decided. Deeper, and more husky. And with an accent that turned her to jelly.

'Quite well, thanks.' Miserable, with heart and other parts aching. But quite well, all things considered. 'How are you, Leo?'

'Very much better for talking to you at last.'

And for the assurance that there was no embarrassing sequel to her visit, thought Harriet bitterly.

'Nonna is writing to you,' he went on.

'Was she very upset? I hope Rosa's news didn't bring on another attack?'

'To my surprise this did not happen. Nonna was astonished, of course. But once the shock of reading Rosa's letter had passed, she became full of curiosity about you, Harriet.'

'Because of the resemblance.'

'Not only that.' He lapsed suddenly into his own tongue. 'Forgive me, but my English is not as good as your Italian, Harriet. I want you to know that Nonna felt so much in sympathy with you she was astonished to find that you are not her granddaughter after all.'

'That's very sweet of her,' said Harriet unsteadily, finding it hard to talk in any language. 'Leo, I must go.'

'Not yet! Not before you give me your number—'

But Harriet could hear her mother coming upstairs and put the phone down, determined to keep her call to Leo secret from Claire. And from Rosa.

Late that night Harriet went slowly through the

ground floor of the house, making sure that everything was spick and span for next day. Enid Morris had had no surviving relatives of her own age, and there would be only a few friends of Claire's and some of the neighbours at the funeral. And Rosa, brushing aside any objections from Claire and Harriet, had insisted on providing refreshments for the occasion from the Chesterton kitchens.

Harriet was locking up for the night when the phone in the kitchen rang. She dived for it before it could wake her mother, then sagged against the wall, her heart thudding at the sound of Leo's voice, speaking in English.

'Harriet? I trust I did not frighten you?'

He sounded both stilted and urgent. An odd combination, she thought, fighting for calm.

'Are you there?' he demanded.

'Yes. I'm here. How did you get the number?'

'It occurred to me that if Nonna was writing to you she must have your address. So I drove to the Villa Castiglione to ask her for it. After that it was simple.'

'Why didn't you just ring your grandmother?'

'I was afraid she might not give me the address without persuasion. Also, I never ring her late at night for fear of startling her.'

'You didn't mind startling *me*.'

'I had no choice.' He paused. 'You do not ask the reason for my call. Are you not curious?'

Of course she was curious! 'I assume you're going to tell me,' she said evenly.

'I wanted you to know that in some ways your news gave me disappointment.'

Harriet's eyes opened wide. 'Have you got the right word?'

'I know my English is not good,' he said impatiently. '*Delusione*, then. Is that clear now?'

She swallowed hard. 'Not really. *Why* are you disappointed?'

'Harriet,' he said patiently, as though speaking to a fractious child, 'if you think about it long enough perhaps you will understand why.'

And to her intense annoyance Leo gave her a taste of her own medicine, and rang off without even saying good-night.

Harriet passed the interminable morning before the funeral by keeping as busy as she could, setting the dining table, putting out the canapés which arrived early from the Chesterton, arranging chrysanthemums and autumn leaves into a centrepiece, and when she ran out of any other chores, fashioning damask napkins into lilies.

Claire came to check on her, looking pale and drawn in a seldom-worn grey suit. 'You needn't bother with that, darling!'

Harriet shook her head. 'No bother—I need occupation. I've put up a snack lunch in the kitchen ready for Kitty and Tim, so there's nothing else to do.'

'You shouldn't have got up so early!'

'Couldn't sleep.' Harriet glanced up from her task at her mother. 'Which makes two of us, I think. Are you feeling rotten, Mother?'

'I'll survive.' Claire smiled brightly. 'Once I see the consultant I'll be fine.'

When Kitty and Chris arrived the atmosphere lightened instantly. Tall and fair and already visibly pregnant, Kitty hugged her mother and sister, then made way for her equally affectionate husband, and from then on time passed so quickly Harriet had to rush in the end to get ready.

After the brief service at the crematorium the family was directed into a sunlit garden to thank the friends who'd come to support them. Harriet shook hands, kissed cheeks, and said all the appropriate things, and at last found herself enveloped in a familiar, scented embrace, as Rosa kissed her and hugged her hard, then drew a familiar figure forward.

'I hope you don't mind, Harriet, but I brought someone with me.'

Harriet stared in utter astonishment at Signora Fortinari, who smiled warmly, then embraced her and kissed the cheeks which had lost colour with shock.

'*Cara,*' she said warmly, 'We did not intrude on the ceremony, of course, but I asked Rosa to bring us here to sympathize with you at this sad time. Will you introduce me to your mother?'

Feeling dazed, Harriet made the necessary introductions to Claire, and Kitty and Tim, then turned in surprise to greet Pascal.

'How sweet of you to come! I didn't know you were back,' said Harriet, receiving his kiss, then turned to Rosa urgently. 'You never said a word about your grandmother, either.'

'I didn't know myself,' protested Rosa. 'Nonna arrived unexpectedly this morning, and insisted on coming with us.'

Harriet turned away for a moment to thank some elderly neighbours, then caught her breath. Colour flooded her pale cheeks, then receded so abruptly that Leo Fortinari, who was waiting with ill-concealed impatience to speak to her, flung out his arms, ready to catch her.

CHAPTER NINE

'I'M NOT GOING TO FAINT,' she said tartly. 'Why didn't you tell me about this last night?'

He took her hand in his. 'I knew you would forbid me to come.'

'But why should she?' demanded Rosa, eyes sparkling. 'Especially if you were talking to her last night, Leo.'

'Because,' said Leo Fortinari, giving his cousin a hostile look, 'Harriet is so embarrassed by the role you forced her to play she will not speak to me.'

Suddenly Harriet realised that the three of them were speaking Italian, and Claire and Kitty, though trying hard not to show it, were agog with curiosity.

Rosa put her arm round Harriet, and smiled at her grandmother, who exclaimed in wonder at the sight of the two faces close together. 'Amazing, isn't it, Nonna? Claire, let me introduce you to my cousin Leo.'

Leo bowed over Claire Foster's hand, and expressed his sympathy. 'I trust we do not intrude on this sad occasion,' he said formally.

Claire assured him she was delighted to welcome both Fortinaris, and insisted that they come back to the house with the other mourners.

He glanced doubtfully at his grandmother. 'We had not thought to stay—'

'We really would like to have you,' said Claire firmly, and gave Leo a wry little smile. 'In the circumstances I'm surprised you were kind enough to come here at all.'

On the car journey back to the house Kitty and Tim were voluble with questions about the Fortinaris, obliging Harriet to give a watered-down version of her trip to Tuscany.

'Rosa Mostyn must have been off her head to think you could carry that off!' commented Kitty bluntly.

'Nevertheless,' said Claire gently. 'Harriet did carry it off, and now Pascal Tavernier has turned up, thankfully, all is explained and no harm has been done.'

Harriet wasn't sure she agreed. Throughout the afternoon, as she served canapés and circulated with drinks, she was conscious all the time of Leo's eyes, which followed her every movement even when he was talking with Pascal and Tim.

'Leo seems bowled over now he's in possession of the facts. In fact, I think my overbearing cousin is totally besotted with you, Harriet,' whispered Rosa in the kitchen at one stage. 'He can't take his eyes off you.'

'It's just seeing you and me together. The resemblance is causing a stir as usual,' muttered Harriet, hefting a tray. 'Open the door for me, please.'

'Resemblance my foot,' scoffed Rosa, following behind with more food. 'He knows which of us is which, believe me. And not just because I'm pregnant. He's the same old supercilious Leo to me, whereas he obviously fancies you like mad, Harriet Foster.'

Once people began to leave Harriet's tension mounted by the minute to the point that after she'd seen the last of the neighbours to the door it was almost a relief to find Leo close behind her in the hall.

'I must speak to you, Harriet,' he said urgently, switching to Italian with obvious relief. 'In private,' he added imperiously.

She frowned. 'Why?'

'If I can be alone with you for a moment I will tell you.'

'It's just not possible,' she whispered. 'When do you go back?'

'In the morning. Nonna is staying on until the wedding.'

'Are you coming back for it?'

'Do you want me to?' He moved nearer.

'That's hardly the point,' she said, standing her ground with difficulty. 'It's Rosa's wedding. She wants you there.'

'If *you* say you want me there, I will come.' He touched a hand to her cheek. 'You are so pale, Harriet.'

'I'm fine,' she assured him, backing away. 'It's been a very hectic time lately.'

'You looked so stunned at the sight of me. Perhaps you are sorry I came,' he said softly, his eyes alight with something which made her knees tremble.

'It was very good of you and your grandmother to take the trouble,' she said formally, pulling herself together.

'Officially I travelled from Fortino to escort Nonna, but in truth I seized the opportunity to see you again. And you have not answered my question,' he pointed out. '*Are* you glad to see me, Harriet?'

'You were so angry with me last time we met I don't see how you can expect me to be,' she retorted.

'There you are!' exclaimed Kitty, popping her blonde head round the drawing room door. 'Time you came and sat down now, Harriet, you've been working like a slave. What can we get you to drink, Leo? We can't rise to a Fortinari Classico, I'm afraid, but Tim's brought some single malt.'

In the drawing room Signora Fortinari was seated close to Claire Foster, talking at length about Rosa's little nephew, and the forthcoming wedding. 'It is not quite the wedding I had in mind,' she said, eyes twinkling. 'I had always hoped that Rosa would marry Leo.'

'But quite apart from all the other drawbacks, Nonna,' said Rosa grinning at Leo. 'We do happen to be first cousins.'

Her grandmother chuckled. 'Ah well. It is all for the best, no doubt. Your Pascal has promised me he will take great care of you instead. And I believe he will.'

'Thank you, Madame,' said Pascal, bowing, and Rosa smiled up at him in such undisguised adoration Leo shook his head in wonder.

'So Harriet was right, Rosa. She told me you had changed a great deal.'

Rosa eyed him narrowly. 'When did she tell you that?'

As sometimes happened in a room where several people are talking at once there was a sudden silence.

'I was talking to Harriet just a moment ago,' said Leo smoothly.

'It must be strange for you, *caro*, now you know she is not Rosa, after all,' observed his grandmother, nodding. 'After her visit to us you must feel you know Harriet better now than you know Rosa.'

'I feel I should mention, Signora,' said Claire with gentle emphasis, 'that Harriet took a great deal of persuading before she consented to the impersonation. Please don't be angry with her.'

'My dear Claire, I am not in the least angry. It was a great surprise to me, I admit.' Signora Fortinari smiled, and held out a hand to Harriet. 'But I hope you will come and visit me again soon as yourself, *cara*. I think I am not mistaken in saying we found great rapport together, you and I.'

Harriet smiled warmly as she clasped the fragile hand. 'Right from the first.'

'Then we shall adopt each other,' said the signora, smiling. She glanced at Claire. 'You will not object?'

'On the contrary, I'll be delighted,' said Claire with obvious relief.

After that the atmosphere in the room grew lighter. Soon Kitty and Rosa were engrossed in discussing antenatal matters, while Signora Fortinari continued her conversation with Claire. Tim and Pascal found a mutual love of rugby football to engross them, at which point Leo gave Harriet a commanding look, and she got to her feet.

'Anyone fancy some coffee?'

'I'll make it,' volunteered Kitty, but Rosa caught her arm.

'Don't worry. Leo will help her,' she said quickly, and won a look of swiftly-veiled gratitude from her cousin as he relieved Harriet of a tray of used plates and glasses.

'Where would you like this?' he asked, and Harriet led the way to the kitchen, her face hot as several pairs of interested eyes followed them.

Once they were in the kitchen Leo dumped the tray down on the table, and caught her hands in his.

'I could not leave without making peace with you,' he said in rapid Italian. 'I have had time since you left to regret my anger towards you, and recognize that it was really fury with myself for taking you against your will.'

'That's not true,' she admitted, her eyes falling. 'In the end I wanted what happened as much as you did. You're probably a very skilled lover.'

'Probably?'

She shrugged. 'How would *I* know?'

Leo smiled suddenly. 'How, indeed!' He tried to look modest. 'I have had no complaints in the past.'

Harriet eyed him wryly. 'Well you wouldn't, would you.'

'What do you mean by that?' he demanded.

'You're Leonardo Fortinari, with looks, a position of importance and a faultless pedigree.' Harriet smiled mockingly. 'What woman in her right senses *would* complain. Except me, of course, and that's different.'

He let out a deep breath, and released her hands. 'I came to talk to you in private to ask if you want me to come to the wedding.'

'Shouldn't you be asking Rosa that?'

'I am asking you!'

'Come, by all means,' she said carelessly. 'And now I really must make that coffee.' She shot a questioning look at him. 'You must think we're an odd family to seem so composed on the day of my grandmother's funeral.'

'No.' Leo sat on the edge of the table to watch as she filled the coffeemaker. 'Your mother is obviously exhausted, and your sister, I think, is not the emotional type.'

'While, as you know, I feel far more affinity for your grandmother than I ever did for mine.' Harriet gave a rueful glance over her shoulder. 'For some reason Grandma never liked me very much.'

'*I* do,' said Leo swiftly. 'You know very well that I am in love with you.'

Innamorato sounded so much more passionate than the English version that Harriet stared at him in astonishment. 'You don't really know me, Leo.' Her hands shook a little as she laid a tray with cups and saucers, hardly aware of what she was doing as he watched her every move.

'I know enough,' he assured her. 'And most important of all, I have the great privilege to be your first lover, Harriet. As I drove back to Fortino from Pisa when you left, it was a thought which occupied my mind to the exclusion of all else. But I was in love with you long before then. I tried hard to fight it, but from the moment I met you at the airport it was difficult to control my desire for the woman I believed to be Rosa.'

Harriet turned away sharply, before he could see how much this declaration delighted her. 'Talking of Rosa, we'd better go back,' she said reluctantly.

Leo sighed deeply, and took the tray from her. 'I wish you could dine with me later, Harriet, but on such a night I know this is impossible. Next week, when I return for the wedding, I shall demand all your time.'

Shortly afterwards Leo had a word with his grandmother, who detached Rosa from Kitty and said it was time to leave.

'You mean we've worn Claire and Harriet out, and probably Kitty, too,' said Rosa penitently.

There were embraces all round, and a promise from Signora Fortinari to visit the Foster household again before the wedding.

'Good-night, my child,' she said, embracing Harriet. 'Take good care of your charming mother. I shall see you soon.'

In the flurry of leavetaking no one noticed that Leo held Harriet's hand so tightly it felt bruised when he released it. She flexed her fingers as she turned back into the house with Claire and Kitty, and accepted gratefully when Tim volunteered to wash up and make tea or pour stiff drinks according to taste.

'Actually,' said Claire, with a sigh, 'When you hear what I have to say I think a stiff drink will be necessary all round.'

Kitty stared in surprise. 'Why, Mother? Something wrong?'

Claire would say no more until the clearing up had been done, by which time Harriet was feeling apprehensive as she sat down with Kitty to listen. Tim, with his usual tact, kissed them all, then went off to watch television.

'I'll relay the news to him in bed,' said Kitty, putting her feet up on the sofa. 'So come on, Mother, we're all ears.'

'First,' said Claire, 'I must apologize to you, Harriet, for behaving like a zombie all week, but it seemed best to get the funeral over with before making my revelations.'

'Revelations?' Kitty prompted. 'What kind?'

After Harriet's departure for Italy, Claire told them, her mother had complained of feeling worse than usual. Taking this as a plea for attention, Claire humoured her by spending more time than usual with her, watching television and reading to her. But late on the Saturday evening Mrs. Morris suddenly told her daughter there was something she must know, and asked for her handbag.

'There was a letter in the zipped part at the back,' said Claire.

'A will?' said Kitty, eyes sparkling. 'Not that she had anything to leave, of course.'

'Stop interrupting, Kit,' said Harriet urgently. 'Let's hear about this letter.'

It had been Enid Morris's intention to leave the letter for Claire to read after her death. But that night it suddenly became vital to her to make a confession which astounded her daughter.

'It was a very strange feeling,' said Claire 'to sit beside my mother and read a letter which informed me that she was not my mother after all.' She gave Harriet a wry little smile. 'In short, I was the one adopted, darling, not you.'

'Good grief!' said Kitty, wide-eyed. 'And Grandma never said a word?'

Claire shook her head. 'I still can't believe it, but it's true.'

Harriet blew out her cheeks in astonishment. 'But you look so much like Grandpa!'

'That's because he actually *was* my father. But this was my birth mother.' Claire took an envelope from her bag, and handed Harriet a photograph of a dark-haired young girl in a long bias-cut dress with flowing georgette sleeves.

'Wow,' said Kitty, peering over her shoulder. 'That could be you, thirties style, sis.'

'What was her name?' said Harriet urgently.

'Chiara Russo.' Claire smiled at her. 'So you're not a freak of nature, after all. Just a throwback to your grandmother.'

According to his wife Harry Morris had met Chiara on one of his many trips to Italy for his firm in the early thirties. To Claire's embarrassment Enid Morris confided that once she was diagnosed as barren she saw no reason to share her bed again with her husband. Which meant that when Harry Morris met Chiara the result was inevitable. When Enid refused to divorce him, Chiara took matters into her own hands and ran away from home, cutting herself off from her family to join her lover in England.

Harriet, who had vague, fond memories of her tall, distinguished grandfather, felt her throat thicken as Claire told how he'd bought a flat in Cheltenham for his love, and because he'd always travelled a lot in his job Enid pretended to see nothing strange in his prolonged absences. But one day he came home in utter despair to say that Chiara had died in childbirth.

'My mother had known all along about Chiara, and at first refused to listen,' Claire went on. 'But when Father told her he had no option but to take the baby to Chiara's family in Italy, Mother had a change of heart. She demanded to see me, found I had fair skin, blue eyes and tufts of red hair and that was that.'

Harriet looked at her quizzically. 'What would have happened if you'd looked like Chiara?'

'I'd have been taken to the unknown Russos in Italy, I suppose.' Claire shrugged ruefully. 'But apparently Mother took one look at me and felt a fierce sense of possession.'

'Which she never lost!' said Harriet.

'I'll say. It's amazing that she ever let you get married,' added Kitty.

Claire smiled. 'Fortunately your father loved me enough to come and live here.'

Kitty looked at the photograph again, then at Harriet, and whistled inelegantly. 'No wonder Grandma never took to you, sis.'

'It's obvious now that Harriet was a constant, living reminder of something my mother wanted forgotten. And my father's fondness for her couldn't have helped, either, nor the fact that I named her for him,' said Claire. 'You were only five when he died, Harriet, so I don't suppose you remember how he doted on you.'

'I do, actually.' Harriet smiled at the memory. 'But looking back on it, I'm sure it was Grandma's attitude that convinced me I was adopted.' She frowned 'But if our grandmother's name was Russo, that doesn't explain my resemblance to Rosa. Her mother was a Fortinari.'

'Just one of life's little mysteries, I suppose,' said Claire, then gave Harriet a troubled look. 'I'm afraid there's more to come. In her will my mother left the house and quite a large amount of money to me, plus five thousand pounds to Kitty.'

'You mean she had money for nurses all along, and you could have had that operation months ago?' said Harriet, outraged.

'That's not the point, darling. She left nothing at all to you.'

Harriet shrugged impatiently. 'I never expected her to—'

'I'll share mine with you,' said Kitty promptly.

'No way, Kit, you keep it for Tim Junior. But

thanks. It was a nice thought.' Harriet jumped up, hugging her arms across her chest. 'What hacks me off is that if Grandma had let Mother have some money for the operation—*and* the repairs, I wouldn't have let Rosa talk me into going to Italy in her place.'

She stopped pacing as she met an identical look in the two pairs of blue eyes watching her. 'What?' she demanded.

'Then you wouldn't have met Leo Fortinari,' said Kitty, forthright as usual. 'And don't try to say you couldn't care less because it was obvious—even to Tim—that you and Signor Fortinari strike sparks off each other.'

Harriet sat down suddenly, thrusting her hair back from her flushed face.

'You're in love with him, aren't you?' asked Claire gently.

'I've only just met him—'

'So what?' said Kitty.

'Until recently he thought I was Rosa,' Harriet pointed out.

'Not any more,' said her mother, smiling. 'In fact it's very obvious that he still looks on Rosa as his naughty little cousin.'

'Can I make a copy of Chiara's photograph?' said Harriet, changing the subject firmly. 'I'd like to keep it.'

'I'd like a copy, too,' said Kitty. 'It's so sad and romantic. Poor little Chiara.' She got up with a sigh. 'I'll make some tea and then I'll take Tim off to bed and tell him the story.'

'I'll make it,' said Harriet, jumping up, but Kitty shook her head, wagging a finger at her as she went to the door.

'Sit!'

Harriet obeyed, exchanging a wry look with her mother. 'No wonder you were so withdrawn all week. This must have come as an enormous shock.'

'It did,' agreed Claire. 'But it explains a lot of things. Mother could be difficult at times, but I know she loved me.'

'That was one thing never in doubt.'

'Apparently there were stipulations on both sides when she agreed to bring me up,' said Claire. 'She insisted Father never told the Russos what had happened, beyond the fact that their daughter had died. No mention was to be made of a child. And Father, in turn, insisted my name must be the English version of Chiara.'

'He really loved her, didn't he?' said Harriet sadly.

'He certainly did.' Claire sighed. 'Poor mother. But she had me as compensation. Her husband's child, but *her* daughter, and that was that. Nevertheless she was unfair to penalize you just because you resembled Chiara. I shall give you some of the money she left me.'

Harriet shook her head. 'I'd much prefer you kept it. Invest it, or blow it all on a cruise—whichever appeals to you most. You've earned every penny of it.' She started up as the phone rang, almost colliding with Tim in the doorway as he came in with a tea tray.

'For you, Harriet,' he said, grinning.

Alone in the kitchen, Harriet bit her lip in disappointment when she found her caller was Rosa.

'Just thought I'd ring to see how you are. I hope you didn't mind when Nonna and Leo came with us today.'

'Of course not. It was very sweet of them.'

'Leo sweet?' Rosa gurgled. 'Sweet on you, maybe.'

'How's Nonna? Sorry, Rosa—'

'What else would you call her? And she's fine, seems to have taken the journey and everything else in her stride. Look, I'll call you tomorrow evening. Give my love to Claire, but don't hang up—someone else wants to talk to you.'

There was a rapid exchange of Italian, then, 'Harriet?' said the familiar, bone-melting voice.

She slid to the floor. 'Hello, Leo, thanks for ringing,' she said in English.

'I know you are tired, but I am leaving too early to call you in the morning. I worried about you today. You looked so pale and tired.'

'I've been busy.'

'And sad, of course. Harriet, I return late on Friday evening, so I shall not see you until the wedding. Rosa tells me you are to be bridesmaid.'

'Which should cause quite a stir,' said Harriet dryly. 'Though it won't be hard to tell us apart.'

'For one thing Rosa is expecting a child, and you are not,' he stated, taking her breath away. 'Besides now that I have seen you together the differences are obvious. Rosa is taller, and her hair is straight, and for her I feel only an impatient affection. For you, *carissima,* I feel something very different.'

'And I know what it is, Leo!' she said hotly. 'You feel responsible for a certain loss of mine. But please don't. It was as much my fault as yours. It doesn't bind you in any way—to anything.'

He said something short and violent in his own tongue, then paused, as though marshalling his forces. 'It is not a subject to discuss on the telephone. We shall continue when we meet face-to-face, Harriet. But now I must let you rest. Please renew my thanks to your mother for her hospitality to Nonna and myself. We did not expect this.'

'Leo—'

'Yes?' he said quickly.

'Before you go could I ask something?'

'Anything you wish.'

'What was your grandmother's name before she was married?'

'Corelli,' he said, surprised. 'Why?'

'Just a matter of interest. Goodbye, Leo.'

'Wait a moment,' he said urgently. 'This loss you speak of—'

'Please—'

'Listen!' he commanded. 'I think of it as a gift you gave into my possession, Harriet. And what I possess, I keep. *Arrivederci, tesoro.*'

CHAPTER TEN

IN THE END, after persuasion from her mother, Harriet took another week off from her job.

'You'll be leaving after Christmas, anyway,' said Claire, 'when you start teaching at Roedale. And to be honest I feel a bit under the weather. I'd appreciate having you home for a while.'

Which settled the matter for Harriet. Her mother rarely pleaded for help, and Harriet felt a lot better when a visit to the gynaecologist confirmed that a simple operation would restore Mrs Foster to full health.

Rosa had paid for the consultation in advance, and wouldn't hear of repayment.

'No,' she said that evening, when she rang to see how Claire had got on. 'It was the deal. I owe it to you, Harriet.'

'But Grandma left Mother quite a bit of money. She wants to contribute.'

'No way. *I'm* footing the bill for the operation, and that's that. Now let's talk frocks.'

Because Rosa felt her grandmother wasn't up to a shopping session, she'd asked the most exclusive dress shop in Pennington to send over a selection of suitable garments to the Hermitage, and Harriet and Claire were bidden to lunch with Rosa and her grandmother to assist in the selection. During the meal, in the signora's private sitting room, Harriet shared a grin with Rosa over the waiter's bemused expression as he served them.

'Poor bloke,' said Rosa, chuckling. 'He couldn't believe his eyes.'

'It will be like that at the wedding, *cara,*' warned Signora Fortinari, 'so choose a dress very different from Harriet's.'

Rosa pulled a face. 'For starters, Nonna, I'm now at least two sizes bigger than Harriet already so that's easy, but there's not much we can do about our faces, unless we wear paper bags over our heads.'

'Different!' said Harriet, chuckling. 'Elegant, shiny bags in toning colours, of course, with holes in the appropriate places—we could start a trend.'

Two hours later a flattering dress in parchment chiffon had been the unanimous choice of everyone for the bride, and a dramatic tawny velvet shift for Harriet.

'Marvellous way to shop,' said Harriet, when tea was served afterwards.

'You can get a personal shopper in lots of places these days,' said Rosa, refusing a cream bun regretfully. 'This was only slightly different.'

'And a very profitable afternoon out for the owner of the shop,' commented Signora Fortinari. She smiled at Harriet. 'You look so much better, *cara.* Leo would be happy to see you with more colour in your face. He was most anxious about you.'

'Tell you what, Nonna,' said Rosa, grinning. 'Now I'm out of the running as a wife for Leo, I think he should marry Miss Foster here.'

'*Rosa!*' said Harriet, almost choking on her tea.

'I think so, too,' said the signora tranquilly. 'They have known each other only a short time, of course, but Leo already has very warm feelings for Harriet, I think. Such a match would please me very much. I shall speak to him.'

Claire eyed her daughter's scarlet face. 'I think Harriet would prefer it if you didn't, Vittoria.'

'Why not, child?' asked the signora in surprise. 'Do you deny you have similar feelings for Leo?'

With three pairs of questioning eyes fixed on her face a downright lie was impossible. 'No,' said Harriet with dignity. 'I like him very much. But nothing more.'

Signora Fortinari smiled indulgently. 'Very well. I shall not interfere.'

Not for the world would Harriet have admitted that she expected to hear from Leo before the wedding, and felt irrationally hurt when he failed to ring. Fortunately it was a busy week. With the novelty of money to spend on clothes for once, Claire took Harriet out on several enjoyable shopping expeditions before she found something to wear to the wedding, also a new dress for the family dinner they were invited to by Tony and Allegra Mostyn on the Friday evening. Leo and Dante would be there, but Mirella was too near her time to travel, and would meet Pascal when he visited Fortino with Rosa during the honeymoon.

Harriet had rather dreaded the celebration dinner, but after the expected, friendly exclamations from Allegra and Tony Mostyn when they were introduced, and a great deal of teasing from the exuberant Dante, the evening started well, with Rosa in tearing spirits.

Leo, to Harriet's secret, burning disappointment, was unable to leave Fortino that day after all.

'He had an important meeting with some Australian wine makers this afternoon, and told me to come on ahead,' said Dante, who was seated next to Harriet in the private dining room reserved for the occasion. 'He told me to tell you he would be here in the morning, and will see you in church.' As his eyes moved from her face to Rosa's, he shook his head in wonder. 'When Leo told me you were not Rosa I could not believe him. It is witchcraft.'

In deference to Claire and Allegra, who had no Italian, the general conversation was conducted in English. And to everyone's amusement Allegra sat with a speaker beside her plate, ready to run if she heard a sound from her son. Fortunately coffee was served before an imperious cry came through.

'Stay there, darling,' said Tony firmly, as his wife shot to her feet. 'I'll bring him down. No one will mind.'

He was assured unanimously that everyone would be only too delighted, and soon after the coffee and brandy were served the proud father reappeared with a small bundle, looking smug.

'I've changed him, and heated the bottle, so over to you, Mummy.'

Allegra received her son with a look of such tenderness for both her men Harriet felt a sharp, unwelcome pang of envy.

'I hear you are to be bridesmaid tomorrow,' said Dante. 'It should make interesting wedding photographs.'

'No problem about who's who—I'll be the one without a bridegroom,' she said flippantly. 'So you don't think I was completely mad to impersonate Rosa, then, Dante?'

'To make my grandmother's birthday perfect? No,' he returned, and squeezed her hand. 'It is very strange to think I must now call you Harriet, and that you are not a cousin after all, alas. But I think you were very brave. Rosa must be grateful to you.' He looked across the table to where Rosa was sitting close to her sister-in-law, her face intent as she watched Allegra feed her baby. 'This Pascal of hers. Will I like him?'

Harriet smiled. 'I do.'

'Then no doubt I shall too.' He looked up as the door opened, then dropped Harriet's hand like a hot cake. '*Allora,*' he said ruefully. 'Leo got away after all.'

Harriet sat motionless, heart thumping, as Tony and Rosa hurried to welcome the late arrival. Leo looked tired, and less immaculate than usual, but one look at him transformed the evening for Harriet. After all the greetings were completed, and he'd paid due homage to the new little Mostyn, he glanced casually at his brother and Dante got up, smiling in resignation, and surrendered his place.

Leo sat beside Harriet and smiled down at her. 'I am late. Forgive me.'

'You should be asking my forgiveness, not Harriet's,' said Rosa, grinning at him. 'So come on, do what you do best, Leo, and give me your orders. What would you like?'

Leo gave his cousin an indulgent smile, but refused food in favour of coffee, while Harriet gathered her wits and tried to think of something interesting to say.

'Good flight?' she asked, cursing her inanity.

'No. It was late.' Leo gave her a look which took in every detail of her face and severe pinstriped dress, the hair she'd twisted up into a loose knot, all of it intended to make her look as different from Rosa as possible. 'You look better, Harriet,' he said, under cover of the general conversation round the table.

'Thank you.'

'Your mother also. How is she coping with her loss?'

'Reasonably well.'

'I did not ring you,' he said in an undertone, 'because I wanted you to miss me.'

Harriet eyed him narrowly. 'I had too much to do to miss you,' she lied. 'I was tied up with Mother's affairs, and Rosa's, of course.'

'Of course.' He cast a resigned eye across the table at his cousin. 'Always it is Rosa. I salute Pascal Tavernier's bravery in taking her to wife.'

'What are you saying about me?' called Rosa across the room.

'I was just saying that Pascal is a lucky man,' said Leo promptly, to Harriet's amusement.

'I think Pascal *is* lucky,' she said in a low tone. 'Contrary to the impression she gives all Rosa wants is a loving, secure relationship, and babies.'

'And *you?*' asked Leo. 'Do you desire the same as Rosa?'

'We all want different things,' she parried, filling his cup with coffee from the pot the waiter had just placed in front of her. She added sugar and passed the cup to him, then looked up to find Rosa and Signora Fortinari watching the process with amusement.

'*Grazie,*' said Leo, and glanced across the room to watch his brother talking to Allegra. 'So Dante kept you entertained before I arrived.'

She nodded. 'Though I really wasn't looking forward to seeing him tonight, nor to meeting Tony and Allegra for the first time. But after the first surprise, everyone's been very tactful and sympathetic.'

'I think Dante would be very much more than sympathetic if you gave him the chance,' said Leo grimly. 'But do not raise hopes you cannot fulfill, Harriet. I utterly forbid you to encourage Dante.'

Harriet gave him a fulminating glare. 'Do you really!'

Fortunately Tony Mostyn chose that moment to get up to make a speech of welcome to all his guests, while waiters circulated with champagne. He had a private word with one of them, then proposed a toast to the bride, and smiled as the waiter returned with a package for Rosa. She took out a single, perfect red rose, and gave a glittering, tearwet smile all round as she announced it was from Pascal.

'I should jolly well hope it is,' said her brother, grinning, and under cover of the general laughter Harriet, still seething about Leo's arrogance, went off to talk to Allegra.

Allegra Mostyn was a small, pretty creature with masses of brown curly hair framing a tired, freckled face, and looked hardly old enough to be married, let alone the mother of bouncing baby son.

'Could I hold him for a moment?' asked Harriet. 'I promise I won't drop him. You look weary.'

'I am a bit—it's past my bedtime.' Allegra surrendered her son carefully, and Harriet sat down beside her, smiling down into the small face.

'Young Huw's obviously going to be a blond six-footer like his Daddy. He's the image of Tony already.'

'Do you think so?' said Allegra, pleased, as Harriet put her finger into the baby's hand and felt the minute fist close in automatic response.

'If you married Leo,' whispered Rosa in her ear, 'you could have one of your own.'

'What is Rosa saying, Harriet, to cause such a ravishing blush?' demanded Dante, coming to join them.

'Girlish confidences, *cugino mio,*' said Rosa blithely. 'My turn to cuddle my nephew now, Harriet. Hand him over—good practice for me.'

Soon afterwards the party began to break up in deference to Signora Fortinari's age.

When Harriet joined her mother to thank Tony for the evening, from the corner of her eye she saw Rosa nod with enthusiasm in response to something Leo was asking her. His eyes sought Harriet's across the room, and with a touch of defiance she held up her face for the kiss Dante planted on both cheeks, then she embraced Signora Fortinari and promised to arrive early next day.

Claire Foster followed suit, then asked Tony if someone could call a taxi to take them back into Pennington.

'No need,' said Rosa cheerfully, hugging Claire and Harriet in turn. 'Leo's driving you home in my car.'

Leo seated Claire beside him, and made general conversation all the way back to the house, which meant that Harriet could do nothing other than to sit in the back and wonder what he had in mind when they arrived. It was obvious he was determined to have time alone with her, though she couldn't see how he was going to achieve this with her mother present.

His method was simple and effective. When they arrived Claire offered coffee Leo refused gracefully, then asked her point-blank if he could have a few moments alone with her daughter.

'I fear I have offended Harriet, Signora,' he said frankly. 'I desire to make my apologies, so that nothing spoils Rosa's day tomorrow.'

Which meant that Claire couldn't have refused even if she'd wanted to. 'Of course, Leo,' she said pleasantly. 'But don't keep Harriet too long. I'll say my good-nights now, and take myself off to bed.'

Once her mother had gone upstairs Harriet went into the sitting room and switched on extra lamps, then stood with arms folded militantly as Leo closed the door behind him.

'If you prefer Dante to me tell me now,' he ordered abruptly.

'To say "prefer" indicates a choice,' she said levelly, answering him in his own tongue. 'Am I to choose one of you, then? And if so, for what, exactly?'

Leo's eyes glittered angrily. 'I cannot answer for Dante but for myself,' he said rapidly, 'I intend to be your lover, Harriet.'

Lover, not husband. Harriet took the blow on the chin, and somehow managed to eye him dispassionately. 'But geographically wouldn't that be rather difficult? I live here. You live in Fortino.'

He frowned. 'You would come to me and share my house, of course.'

Harriet's eyes flashed. 'Would I really! Wouldn't your grandmother disapprove? Your parents, too, for all I know.'

'Harriet, I am a grown man. I please myself.' He

spread his hands. 'If you *had* been Rosa, of course, it would be different.'

'But because I'm not a Fortinari,' said Harriet in precise, cutting English, 'it's all right to cut to the chase and not bother about preliminaries like a wedding ring.'

His eyes narrowed. 'But you told me very clearly that you had no wish for marriage.'

Harriet ground her teeth. Surely the man realised she'd been referring to the shotgun variety! 'I meant marriage for the wrong reasons.'

Leo moved closer. 'And for you what are the right reasons, Harriet?'

'The usual ones.' Like wanting to spend every minute of the rest of her life with the man she loved, aka Leo Fortinari. 'Of course,' she added coolly, 'I realise that your religion makes choosing a wife a serious business, though if the bride can bring a couple of handy vineyards to the union it obviously adds to her charms where you're concerned.'

'True,' he admitted, enraging her.

'So love doesn't come into it?' she demanded.

'If one is fortunate, yes.' His eyes darkened. 'I want you, Harriet, and I mean to have you. However, since you have no wish for marriage, I have no objection to a less formal arrangement.'

She stared at him incredulously. 'No *objection*? You could be discussing some business deal. I thought you Latins were supposed to be a hot-blooded bunch.'

'You doubt my passion for you?' he said menacingly, and seized her in his arms and kissed her with a passion which confirmed, beyond all doubt, that the blood in his veins was as hot as any woman could desire. And desire him Harriet did, instantly, as he picked her up and sat down on a sofa with her, cradling her against him as he went on kissing her in a way which quickly brought both of them to fever pitch.

'*No!*' gasped Harriet, making a superhuman effort to free herself.

Leo got up and held out his hand to pull her to her feet. 'You deny this feeling between us, Harriet?' he panted. 'Ah, *carissima*. I will take such pleasure in teaching you about love.'

'You mean sex,' she retorted furiously, and pulled her trembling hands away. 'Sorry, Leo, the answer's no. You're too fond of the word forbid.'

The tension left Leo's face abruptly. 'Ah. This is why you refuse me. You are still angry because I forbade you to encourage Dante.'

'True. Though that's nothing to do with turning down your gracious proposition,' she said with sarcasm.

'So *why* are you refusing me?' he demanded.

Harriet went to the door and opened it pointedly. 'Think about it, Leo, and perhaps you'll find the answer.'

Leo shut it again, and stood with his back to it. 'Tell me why you refuse. Now.'

'No.'

'Then I must give you all the reasons why you should accept,' he went on, unperturbed, and leaned, relaxed, against the door. 'You cannot hide your response to me when I make love to you, therefore you do not find me unattractive. You love my country, you like my house, and I have the means to keep you in comfort— your mother also, should this be a problem for you.'

Harriet gave him a startled look. 'My mother?'

'Of course,' he assured her. 'You know that I desire you,' he went on, 'and I believe, no matter how much you deny this, that your feelings are similar towards me.' His eyes lit suddenly with a gleam which quickened her pulse. 'If we were alone, I would take you to bed and convince you in the best way known to man and woman that we would find joy together.'

'Which is what you did when you thought I was Rosa!' she retorted.

Leo spread his hands in the gesture she was beginning to know so well. 'No, you are mistaken. I did this to make you admit you were *not* Rosa. I had my suspicions from the start. Which is why I kept asking questions—'

'About the cherubs on the ceiling, and Luisa Bracco's marital status,' said Harriet bitterly. 'If you had doubts all along why didn't you voice them?'

Leo moved away from the door. 'Because I was intrigued. I knew that Rosa had no sister. So as the weekend progressed I tried to persuade myself that Rosa had grown into a mature, beautiful woman very different from the girl who had caused so much trouble in the past.'

Harriet backed away slightly. 'The way I heard it you were the one who kept Nonna and Rosa apart.'

Leo's mouth twisted. 'I am not proud of that.'

'Why did Rosa get all the blame, and not Guido Bracco?' demanded Harriet.

'I punished the boy very severely,' he reminded her. 'But if you remember Rosa as she was at seventeen, she was temptation incarnate. She was very definitely to blame. Guido was no match for her wiles.'

'While all she wanted was *your* attention, Leo.' Harriet sighed. 'Poor Rosa.'

'I can feel sympathy for her now. But at the time I blamed Rosa for everything that went wrong in my life.'

'So you did love Luisa!'

'I know now that I did not. But I thought I did then.'

'So why on earth didn't you make it up with her?' demanded Harriet.

'Pride,' he said curtly. 'When Luisa flung her ring at me I caught it, turned my back and walked away.'

Harriet could picture the scene only too clearly. 'So she married someone else.'

'Yes, which did nothing to soothe my pride,' he said sardonically. 'But that was a long time ago.'

'Perhaps you could still get together,' suggested Harriet tartly.

'I did consider it fleetingly,' he agreed, taking the wind out of her sails.

She scowled. 'Those tempting vineyards again.'

Leo smiled slowly. 'As you say, those tempting vineyards. To be truthful, when Nonna invited her to the party I had some vague intention about reconciliation. Then you arrived, and I had no more thoughts about Luisa, or anyone else.'

'Just Rosa,' she said flatly.

'In my heart of hearts, my beautiful Harriet, I always knew you were not Rosa. My mind told me this was impossible. But my heart knew better.'

Harriet looked at him doubtfully, longing to believe him. 'Is that why you made love to me?'

Leo met her eyes without evasion. 'When I carried you off to bed my plan was to find out if you were really Rosa. If you were not, I reasoned, you would not allow it. But in the end I desired you so fiercely who you were became irrelevant. My only regret is that you did not share the ultimate ecstasy I experienced in your arms.'

Harriet's face reddened, then paled so suddenly Leo leapt towards her.

'Don't worry,' she said swiftly, stepping out of reach. 'I'm not about to swoon in true maidenly fashion.'

'But you are tired, *carissima*,' he said in remorse, the tenderness in his voice thickening her throat.

'Yes,' she admitted huskily, 'I am. And tomorrow is Rosa's wedding day. I really must get to bed.'

'I would give much to carry you there, and hold you in my arms all night, Harriet,' he said caressingly. 'I will go now, but this discussion is not finished. I know, beyond all doubt, that we were meant to be together.'

'But then, Leonardo,' she retorted, deliberately mocking to hide the tumult inside her, 'to quote your grandmother, you are not always right.'

Leo seized her in his arms, looking down at her with eyes lambent with a confidence which some secret, traitorous part of her responded to shamelessly. 'In this case, *cara mia*, I am most definitely right.' His mouth met hers in a kiss of such unexpected tenderness Harriet had no defence against it. He tensed, his arms tightening as the kiss deepened and grew more passionate, until they were both breathing raggedly when he let her go. 'I want you, Harriet,' said Leo huskily, 'and I mean to have you. *Buona notte*— I shall see you in church.'

CHAPTER ELEVEN

To prevent her own problems from spoiling Rosa's wedding day, Harriet set out to enjoy it with only slightly less enthusiasm than the bride.

'Do I look fat?' demanded Rosa, twisting and turning in front of a mirror in her own private apartment at the Hermitage.

'Do you care?' countered Harriet, as she zipped the pale, frothing chiffon into place.

'No. Not a bit.' Rosa grinned, then took Harriet's hand so that they stood together before the long cheval glass. 'The heavenly twins—more or less.' She turned to Harriet and embraced her suddenly. 'I refuse to cry and spoil this expensive make-up, but I wish we'd got together years ago. You know how much I appreciate your friendship—and Claire's. Promise me you'll come and visit me soon in Paris.'

Harriet held her close. 'Of course I will. But not for a while. Pascal will want you to himself for a bit.' She put Rosa away gently. 'Come on, bride, let's find Nonna and my mother, see if they approve.'

But Rosa held back. 'First, Harriet, can I ask you something?'

'Depends what it is.'

'How *did* Leo find out you weren't me?' Rosa stared, wide-eyed, as colour rose in Harriet's face. 'Oh dear, what have I said?'

'He suspected from the first,' said Harriet gruffly.

150

'Kept trying to trip me up. But in the end he found out something which clinched it.'

'How?'

Harriet hesitated, then looked Rosa in the eye. 'He made love to me. I tried to stop him but I couldn't.'

'*What?* You mean Leo *forced* you?' demanded Rosa fiercely.

'Absolutely not! He simply set out to prove I wasn't you. Assumed that if I was someone else I would object. I did, at first, but in the end I couldn't. I was just—carried away. We both were.'

'Wow, so that's it! No wonder he looks like a hungry tiger whenever he's near you.' Rosa frowned. 'But I still don't get it, Harriet. What made him realise you weren't me? We checked we had no birthmarks, and so on—you're blushing again!'

Harriet stared down at the tips of her tawny velvet shoes. 'It was the first time for me,' she muttered, then looked up at last to meet the astonishment in Rosa's eyes. 'Go on. Laugh if you like.'

'You're kidding!' Rosa shook her head in awe. 'Glory be. How on earth did Leo react?'

'Predictably. He was furious. At first, anyway.'

'He certainly isn't any more.' Rosa's eyes narrowed suddenly. 'Oh dear. You've been looking awfully peaky since you came back. Don't tell me he's made you pregnant!'

'No.' Harriet smiled. 'Though oddly enough he was the first one to think of that. Afterwards.'

'Leo, being Leo, would have insisted on doing the honourable thing if you had been, you know.'

Harriet pulled a face. 'I do know. But fortunately he wasn't obliged to. Besides, I told him marriage doesn't appeal to me.'

Rosa groaned in despair. 'What did you tell him *that* for?'

'Because his first reaction was to accuse me of trying to trap him,' said Harriet, eyes flashing at the memory.

'No!' Rosa whistled inelegantly. 'But he's obviously changed his tune a bit since then.'

'Yes, he has,' said Harriet lightly. 'Just between you and me, Rosa, Leo would be very happy with a less formal relationship.'

Rosa's jaw dropped. 'Leo asked you to be his mistress?'

Harriet laughed outright. 'Nothing so fancy, you muggins. He just asked me to move in with him. As people do.'

Rosa shook her head. 'Not anywhere near Nonna they don't. At least, not if they're Fortinaris. They marry.'

'Preferably if the bride comes complete with vineyards! Come on, time to go.'

It was impossible for any guest present to feel anything but happiness for Rosa as she married Pascal Tavernier at a small country church near the Hermitage, the expression on their two faces as they said their vows bringing tears to more than one pair of eyes in the congregation. And afterwards, in a private dining room at the Hermitage, there was music from a trio, and much laughter and champagne as the bride and groom received the kisses and congratulations of their guests.

'You are dazzling today,' said Leo, once he'd managed to detach Harriet from a group of Pascal's relatives. 'Also very clever. Rosa is fortunate to have so multilingual a bridesmaid.'

'But you can indulge me and speak English!' Harriet accepted the glass of champagne he procured for her. 'I must find my mother—'

'Your mother is talking to a Frenchman who not only speaks English, but is obviously charmed with her company. Stay with me for a while, *tesoro,*' ordered Leo. 'Have you thought any more about my suggestion?' he said abruptly.

Harriet had thought of little else. 'Yes,' she said, lifting her glass in toast to Allegra across the room.

Leo drew her to a quiet corner and stood over her, looking down into her face. Rosa had requested no formality for her wedding, and Leo was wearing a suit which fitted his elegant frame with such casual perfection Harriet had no doubt it had been made for him. And his tie, she noticed, raising an eyebrow, was almost the exact shade of her dress.

Leo smiled as he intercepted her look. 'I asked,' he said simply. 'Harriet. *Carissima.* I want you so much. Come back with me to Fortino.'

She shook her head firmly. 'No, Leo.'

'Why not?' he demanded, scowling.

'I can't tell you here—'

'Then come to my room later,' he said urgently. 'No one will miss us for an hour.'

'Certainly not,' she said incensed. 'What do you take me for?'

He threw out his hands. 'How else can we achieve private discussion?'

'You've forgotten my mother,' she pointed out.

'Nonna wishes her to remain after the reception,' said Leo, as if that settled it. 'I shall drive you both home later. After we have spent time alone together,' he added very deliberately.

Harriet gave him a long, considering look. 'I must go. Rosa wants me.'

'Always Rosa,' he retorted impatiently.

'Without Rosa we would never have met,' she reminded him.

'Then I shall escort you to her and kiss the bride with much gratitude,' said Leo promptly, then gave her a narrowed, warning look. 'But I insist you spend time in my room with me once she has gone.'

But after the bride and groom had left in a hail of confetti for their flight to Venice, Leo Fortinari found that for once in his life he was forced to admit defeat. Tony Mostyn had ordered a late supper for all the guests, and his secretly fuming cousin could find no way to refuse without offending their grandmother, and risking another rift between the Fortinaris and the Mostyns.

The other obstacle to his plan was Harriet's unspoken opposition to it. Furious with Leo for assuming she would go off with him so publicly, she made sure her mother was happy with Signora Fortinari and Pascal's uncle, then joined Dante and some of Pascal's cousins, and abandoned Leo to the more senior group of guests.

After the meal was over Leo came to join her immediately, looking like thunder, but Harriet steadfastly refused to allow him to detach her from the group, knowing perfectly well what he would demand if she did. Ignoring the urgency she could feel radiating from him, Harriet laughed and chatted until her smile felt pasted on her face by the time Claire came to join them.

'Harriet, I've got a lift. Jean Tavernier's offered to

drive me home. Are you coming, or will you stay awhile?'

'I'll come with you, Mother,' said Harriet quickly, before Leo could say a word, quailing inwardly at the look in his eyes when she said goodbye to him in full view of everyone. Stony-faced he stood rigid alongside Dante as Harriet took Claire's hand to circulate among the guests, then embraced Signora Fortinari with much affection.

When they reached the Fortinari brothers Leo took graceful leave of Claire Foster then turned to Harriet.

'*Arrivederci*,' said Leo, and kissed her hand very correctly.

Harriet quailed inwardly at the look in his eyes as he straightened, then surrendered her hand for Dante's kiss, and without looking again at Leo went off with her mother and Pascal's uncle.

Amazed that she'd had the strength, and the face, to leave Leo flat so publicly, Harriet sat in the back of the car on the way home, aware that her mother and Jean Tavernier were talking animatedly, but quite beyond contributing anything herself. Normally she would have found it amusing that this time it was she who went up to bed and left her mother to entertain the charming Monsieur Tavernier. But all she could manage were polite thanks for the lift home, and instructions to Claire that if anyone rang she was in bed. Asleep.

Harriet got ready for the night in utter misery, her reasons not nearly so clear by this stage for turning Leo's offer down. Deep down, she forced herself to admit, she'd hoped that her objection to becoming his lover would turn his thoughts to marriage. Fond hope that had been! And now, by comparison to a life without Leo, a less formal arrangement sounded a whole lot more attractive than no arrangement at all. But regrets were pointless. Remembering his reaction to Luisa Bracco's rejection, Harriet faced the truth. Leo's pride would never allow him to contact her again.

She was right. There were phone calls next day from Dante and Signora Fortinari, but none from Leo. Harriet learned that all three of them were flying back to Italy that afternoon, and promised the Signora that one day she would go back to the Villa Castiglione, and this time bring Claire with her. Afterwards Harriet was sorely tempted to ring the Hermitage and ask for Leo. But in the end she put the phone back, firmly convinced a receptionist would inform her that Mr Fortinari refused to speak to Miss Foster.

The time following Rosa's wedding was very strange. Without Enid's presence the big old house seemed very empty to both Harriet and Claire, and without Rosa to enliven it, or the prospect of seeing Leo again, Harriet found life in general unbearably empty. At last, unable to hide her unhappiness from her anxious mother she gave her the details of her rift with Leo, only to be astonished by Claire's reaction.

'I don't want to lose you, darling, but you're obviously madly in love with Leo. What's the point in being miserable here, when you could be happy with him in Fortino?'

'That's the point. Fortino. Just between you and me, Mother dearest, if Leo had proposed playing house together here in Pennington I might have said yes.' Harriet sighed heavily. 'But in Fortino it just isn't on. There's the Signora for a start. And Rosa says Leo's mother's a pretty formal lady, too.' And the mere thought of the reaction from people like Sophia Rossi turned Harriet cold. 'I'm more conventional than I thought,' she said miserably.

Soon afterwards Claire was admitted to hospital, and within a very short time after the operation looked so much better Harriet realised how much her mother's condition had been pulling her down. And shortly afterwards the builders arrived to start on the house repairs. Time to sweep the cobwebs of the past away, Claire told her daughter.

Some cobwebs, however, proved very persistent. It astonished Harriet that a man she'd known for so short a time could leave such a large hole in her life. She heard news of Leo from time to time, since Signora Fortinari, of the generation who liked writing letters, wrote regularly with news of Mirella, who was growing very large, and Dante who was as lively as ever, and Leo, who was working much too hard. And Harriet wrote back, to say that Claire's operation was a great success and the house was in turmoil, but found it hard to find anything else of interest to relate.

One evening Harriet was hanging curtains in the newly-decorated drawing room, with Claire holding the ladder steady, when the phone rang.

'Kitty always rings at the wrong moment,' said Harriet, laughing. 'Go on, answer it. I promise I won't slip.'

But when Claire came back and said Leo wanted her Harriet nearly fell flat on her face. 'What does he want?' she demanded, as her mother held the ladder for her to climb down.

'No idea, darling. But he sounds pretty stressed.'

'Nonna?'

'Go and find out!' ordered Claire, and Harriet flew to the kitchen.

'Leo?' she said breathlessly.

'Harriet, have you been running?' he demanded.

'No. I was up a ladder. Hanging curtains. Something must have happened for you to ring me. What's wrong?'

'Mirella fell at the Villa Castiglione this morning—'

'*Please* don't say she lost the baby?'

'No she has not. Harriet, listen!' he ordered. 'Mirella is well, and Franco can take her home tomorrow, but Nonna was so shocked by the accident that she is confined to bed. I am very worried about her.'

'Oh Leo, I'm so sorry. Is she in hospital, too?'

'No, at home. I have hired a nurse.'

'Thank you for letting me know.'

'I rang to say more than this.'

Her heart leapt. 'Go on.'

'Nonna refuses to interrupt Rosa's honeymoon, and wants you to come to her instead.' He paused. 'Will you, Harriet?'

Harriet swallowed hard on her disappointment. 'Yes, of course. But it would have to be at the weekend. I can't take any more time off.'

'You should come immediately, Harriet,' he said, startling her.

'Then of course I will.'

'I will reimburse you for any money you lose by taking leave from your job.'

'Certainly not,' she said frigidly.

'As you wish. I took the liberty of booking a flight

for you in the morning,' he informed her, and gave her details. 'I will meet you at Pisa.'

The following hours were a mad scramble of hair washing and last-minute ironing, and lamentations on Harriet's part that she'd had no time for shopping.

'Last time I went kitted out in borrowed glory,' she said gloomily, thrusting trousers and sweaters into a suitcase.

'This time you're going as yourself,' her mother reminded her. 'The signora won't mind what you wear as long as you turn up. I wonder why she wants to see you? Did Leo say how serious it is?'

'Only that I should go now instead of at the weekend,' said Harriet anxiously.

This time Harriet found Leo waiting for her as soon as she got off the plane. He looked tired and strained, and her heart leapt at the sight of him. For a moment she was sure he would take her in his arms, but instead he took her hand, and to her dismay shook it very formally, as though they were strangers.

'Thank you for coming, Harriet.'

'How are Nonna and Mirella?' she asked anxiously.

'Because you are coming Nonna says she feels better, and Mirella will be home later this afternoon. My mother is going with Franco to fetch her, but she will be at the Villa first to greet you,' he said, unaware of the effect this news had on Harriet. He eyed the luggage carousel. 'Which is yours?'

Harriet pointed out the battered holdall of her student days, and Leo collected it and led the way outside to the car.

'It is good of you to come so swiftly.'

'Not at all.'

He glanced at her, then returned his attention to the road. 'Nonna says your mother made a good recovery after her operation.'

'Yes, she's fine now. I left her preparing for the daily session with the builders. The house repairs are in full swing.'

'Ah, yes. It was Rosa's offer to pay for these that persuaded you to come in her place, of course,' he observed coldly.

Harriet ground her teeth. 'Tony Mostyn sent the builders to us, but Mother's paying for the repairs herself. My grandmother left her some money.' From the corner of her eye she saw Leo's mouth tighten.

'I apologize,' he said tightly. 'It is, of course, no concern of mine.'

Message received, loud and clear, thought Harriet furiously, and relapsed into silence neither of them broke until they were almost at the Villa.

'Leo, please tell me the truth,' said Harriet, at last. 'Nonna's not dying is she?'

'Not yet,' he assured her. 'But ill enough that if she expresses a wish we all do our best to fulfil it. She wanted you to come. So I passed on the request. Even though,' he added, with sudden, startling bitterness, 'you made it plain last time we met that you prefer to avoid all future encounters with me.'

Before Harriet could tell him how hopelessly wrong he was he had stopped the car. A slim regal woman came out onto the loggia to greet them, and Harriet got out quickly, bracing herself for the meeting with Signora Maria Fortinari.

Leo collected Harriet's bag and led her up the steps. 'Mamma, this is Harriet Foster.'

'I can see that for myself.' His mother shook her

head in open amazement. 'Extraordinary! I met Rosa and her husband recently, of course. Otherwise I would have sworn you were my niece, Miss Foster.'

'Harriet is smaller than Rosa, also her hair curls,' said Leo curtly, winning a strange look from his mother.

'How do you do, Signora,' said Harriet, holding our her hand. 'How is your mother? And Mirella too, of course. It was a shock when Leo rang.'

Maria Fortinari held on to Harriet's hand for a moment or two, then smiled with a warmth which had been lacking in her son's welcome. 'My daughter is fine, and my mother-in-law is improving, and will improve even more now you are here, I fancy. I shall go with Franco to collect Mirella later. And now you are here to keep Nonna company I can leave her without worrying. It is difficult to be in two places at once.'

As they entered the house, Silvia came bustling from the kitchen in smiling welcome. 'The Signora is sleeping, so I shall bring tea. The nurse will tell us when she is ready for visitors.'

It was strange to sit on the faded ruby velvet under the familiar cherubs, but this time in company with a woman whose resemblance to her son was so marked that Harriet would have known her anywhere.

'Can you stay, Leo?' asked his mother. 'Or must you get back to Fortino?'

'It will survive without me a little while longer,' he said indifferently.

'You have had a very eventful time lately, Miss Foster,' said Maria Fortinari, looking amused.

Harriet smiled ruefully. 'Very. You know, of course, that Rosa persuaded me to come here in her place, but it seems quite extraordinary to me, now, that I ever had the audacity to do it.'

'Leo tells me you yielded to very powerful persuasion from Rosa. Besides, it made my mother-in-law very happy on her special birthday, so I, for one, can only thank you. But Leo, how will you explain to our friends that Harriet is not Rosa after all?'

'In the unlikely event that anyone should broach the subject with me,' said her son with hauteur, 'I shall refuse to discuss it.'

'When Dante returns from California I can see I shall have to rely on him for tactful explanations!' said his mother wryly.

'As always,' retorted Leo, then jumped up to relieve Silvia of a heavily-laden tea tray.

'I brought coffee for you, Signor Leo,' she panted, and he thanked her, smiling at her with the first sign of warmth since Harriet's arrival.

While she poured, Leo's mother made it plain she was fascinated by the resemblance to Rosa. 'Forgive me if I stare,' she declared, eyeing Harriet over her cup. 'I had not seen Rosa for many years, of course, until recently, but hers—and yours—are not the type of beauty one forgets. Yet Leo informs me there is no connection.'

Harriet hesitated. 'In actual fact,' she said, avoiding Leo's eyes, 'I've recently learned about some Italian ancestry, which probably accounts for the colouring.'

'How interesting—' Maria Fortinari broke off as Silvia came in to say that there was a friend of the Signora's on the line, asking about the invalid. Maria excused herself and went out, and to give herself something to do Harriet refilled her teacup.

'Would you like more coffee?' she asked politely,

and Leo thanked her and held out his cup. Harriet filled it, added sugar and handed the cup back, inordinately pleased with the steadiness of her hand.

'You never mentioned your Italian blood,' commented Leo.

'I didn't know until a short time ago.'

'You have lost weight, Harriet,' he said abruptly.

'Thank you.'

'It was not meant as a compliment!'

She smiled faintly. 'Then I take my thanks back. Though since you brought the subject up, I think you look thinner too.'

'Which is no mystery. I work hard,' he said morosely.

'But that's nothing new, is it?'

'I work longer hours.'

'Are you short-staffed?' she asked politely.

His eyes glittered malevolently. 'No. I am not. I fill my time with work to forget the way you so publicly humiliated me.'

Her eyes flashed. 'I didn't care for the proposition you made.'

He got up restlessly. 'It is not one I have ever made to any other woman.'

'In the circles you move in here in Fortino I don't suppose it is!' she snapped, then subsided quickly as his mother came into the room.

'The invalid is asking for you, my dear,' she said, smiling. 'Don't let her keep you too long. You must be hungry. We shall lunch together when you come down.'

Harriet went up the familiar stairs to the Signora's room, and tapped on the half-open door. A serene-faced woman in a crisp white uniform beckoned her in, smiling.

'Signorina Foster, my name is Claudia. Do come in. I shall leave you alone with the Signora for a while.'

In trepidation Harriet went over to the bed, expecting the worst, then smiled joyfully as she saw Vittoria Fortinari sitting up against piled pillows in a frivolous lace bedjacket, her colour remarkably good.

'Nonna!' said Harriet unsteadily, and felt her eyes fill with tears as she bent to kiss the soft, lined cheek. 'You look wonderful.'

'I am wonderful, now you are here, child.' The invalid returned the kiss with enthusiasm, then patted the bed beside her. 'Sit down and tell me all about Claire, then tell me why you've made my grandson so miserable none of us dares speak to him without incurring his wrath.'

Harriet laughed, blew her nose and wiped her eyes, then drew up a small wicker chair. 'I'd better sit here. Your bed is so perfect I daren't perch on it.' She felt giddy with relief. Far from close to death's door as she'd dreaded, Signora Fortinari looked amazingly well as she explained that Mirella's fall had frightened everyone badly.

'I had a little turn. But as I am sure you can tell, now you have met her, Maria is equal to all crises,' said the Signora, with a wicked little smile. 'In no time the doctor was here, and Mirella was in the hospital, with no harm done, thank the good God. Before I could say a word Leo had arranged for Nurse Claudia to come and I was put to bed and made to stay here. So I took advantage of the situation and insisted he sent for you.'

Harriet couldn't help laughing. 'Leo frightened me out of my wits when he rang. I was hanging curtains and almost fell off the ladder.'

The invalid smiled affectionately. 'Forgive me for worrying you, dearest.'

'Now I know you're all right I don't mind in the least,' said Harriet truthfully.

The signora eyed Harriet's coiled hair and neat navy business suit without enthusiasm. 'Change into something comfortable, then go and have some lunch,' she ordered, 'and take your hair down. You look like a nun.'

'Yes, ma'am!' said Harriet, saluting smartly. 'See you later.'

In Rosa's old bedroom she took a quick shower, pulled on brown velveteen trousers and a pink cashmere sweater Claire had insisted on buying for her. Harriet added a few touches to her face, brushed out the hair which had grown long enough to curl on her shoulders, then ran back to Signora Fortinari's room for approval.

'Is this better?' she demanded, and the invalid smiled with satisfaction and kissed her fingers to her.

'Beautiful. Now run along to Maria and eat some lunch. You are too thin.'

Harriet laughed, then hurried back along the gallery to the stairs and ran down to the hall, almost colliding with Leo in the process. He held her steady, his fingers biting into her arms, then with a choked sound he bent his head to kiss her with a hunger he so obviously couldn't control Harriet felt a surge of elation before she summoned the will to push him away.

CHAPTER TWELVE

DURING LUNCH MARIA Fortinari made it clear that Harriet was not expected to spend all her time with the invalid. 'The nurse will make sure my mother-in-law rests as much as possible and Claudia must have time to herself, of course. But so must you.'

'I'll be glad to sit with Nonna—' Harriet bit her lip, flushing, and Maria smiled.

'Do not feel embarrassment, my dear. Vittoria told me she has adopted you as an extra granddaughter, so how else would you speak of her?' She glanced at her morose son. 'Is something wrong with the meal, Leo?'

He looked at his plate as though he'd only just discovered it was there. 'Nothing at all,' he said blankly, and began to eat.

Maria Fortinari was too accomplished a hostess to allow conversation to flag, and firmly drew her son into the conversation as she asked after Claire's health and questioned Harriet on her life in Pennington, and said Dante was enjoying a well-earned holiday. But Harriet was glad when Franco arrived in so great a rush to get to his wife he barely had time to greet the visitor warmly, before taking his mother-in-law away to collect Mirella.

'It is too cold to go out on the loggia,' said Leo brusquely, once the others had left. 'We shall drink coffee in the salon.'

'Look, Leo,' said Harriet, nettled by his tone.

166

'You're obviously anxious to get back to Fortino. You don't have to stay on my account.'

Leo got to his feet quickly, his face dark with anger. 'If you do not require my presence then of course I shall relieve you of it.' He strode from the room, and a moment later Harriet, utterly dismayed, heard the Maserati roar into life before it took off in a manner more like Dante than Leo.

Silvia came in with a tray, then halted, looking blank as she found Harriet alone.

'The others had to leave,' said Harriet, forcing a smile. 'I'll just drink my coffee, then I'll go for a walk in the garden.'

'Nurse Claudia says her patient must rest for a while,' said Silvia, putting the tray down. 'She will take her lunch now in the kitchen, and will tell you later when you can return to see the Signora.'

Harriet thanked her, then downed two cups of coffee in quick succession, in sudden desperate need for caffeine. What a fool she'd been to nourish hopes of hurling herself into Leo's arms, all differences solved the moment they met. In your dreams, Foster, she told herself scornfully, and went up to her room to collect a jacket. By the time Nurse Claudia called her in from her walk Harriet had resigned herself to the fact that however much Leo might want her for a lover, as a wife she remained ineligible due to a sad lack of vineyards like Luisa, or Mostyn money like Rosa.

Upstairs with the remarkably lively invalid Harriet did her best to put Leo from her mind, and found it no hardship to sit talking with his grandmother. Once they had exhausted the subject of Rosa's wedding, Mirella's accident and Claire's health, Vittoria gave her companion a searching look.

'So tell me, dear, are you happy?'

Harriet frowned, surprised, and took time to answer. 'It depends on what you mean by happy, Nonna.'

'I mean in the way that Mirella and Rosa are happy,' said Vittoria simply. 'I would like to see *you* happy in that way also, child.'

'If you mean with Leo, not a chance,' said Harriet bluntly, 'he doesn't care for me in that way.'

'And what way is that?'

'As Franco does for Mirella, and Pascal for Rosa.'

'Ah. You mean as a husband.'

Harriet nodded. 'Exactly. Now then, Nonna, would you like me to read to you?'

The time passed in a strangely restful way until the evening. Now that she had met Leo again, and found that there was no fairy-tale solution to their estrangement after all, Harriet shut him from her mind and concentrated on his grandmother. And the time passed so pleasantly she felt no qualms when Maria Fortinari rang at one point to say that if all was well with her mother-in-law she would like to stay with Mirella for a day or so.

'I have asked Leo to call at the Villa regularly to check on you, Harriet, and I shall ring for a chat now and then,' she added. 'We are all very grateful to you. Please ring me here at Mirella's if you have the slightest anxiety about anything. She hopes to see you when she is back on her feet. I shall come for you. Please give my love to Vittoria and tell her all is well with Mirella and the baby.'

While Signora Fortinari ate a light supper Harriet kept her company to allow Nurse Claudia time to eat her own meal downstairs with Silvia. Wishing she could have had her own meal with them, Harriet went downstairs later to the dining room to find it set for two, and Leo waiting to pull out her chair for her.

'My mother thought you would like company for dinner,' he said, eyeing her stunned face. 'But if you prefer to eat alone, Harriet, I can return to Fortino.'

Harriet managed a polite smile. 'Of course not. I'm glad you could join me.'

It was all very well in theory, she found, as she began on a slice of golden melon, to decide to shut Leo Fortinari from her life. In practice, facing him across the table, it was another matter entirely. Instead of one of his formal suits he wore a black sweater and trousers with a blue shirt, and, despite the marks of fatigue under his eyes, looked too strikingly attractive for Harriet's hard-won peace of mind.

'My mother returned from California early to be with Mirella,' he said conversationally, 'but my father remained behind to tour various wineries in the Napa Valley, and Dante has gone to join him. He will be sorry to have missed you.'

'Does it make life harder for you at Fortino without Dante?' she asked politely.

Leo put down his fork, his eyes locked with hers. 'It is not Dante's absence which makes my life harder.'

For a moment tension crackled in the air between them, then Leo looked up with a smile as Silvia brought in the main course. When she had gone Leo asked, with determined courtesy, how Harriet had spent her time with Nonna.

'It's no hardship to keep her company,' Harriet assured him. 'She's been telling me about you and Dante and Mirella when you were young, and about the entertaining she used to do at Fortino while your grandfather was alive.'

'She was very beautiful when she was younger,' he said, his eyes softened. 'You must see her photographs. She has several albums of them somewhere. I'll look for them after dinner.'

From then on the evening was less strained. Harriet drew Leo out about his work at Fortino, listening raptly as he described the constant search for perfection for the Fortinari label.

'And you, Harriet,' he said, over coffee later. 'Are you looking forward to your teaching job next year?'

'Not a lot,' she said honestly. 'I'm fortunate to fill in at my old school for a couple of terms, but I only took the job to be at home with my mother for a while. I shall apply for something farther afield next.'

'And what will your mother do then?'

'She has her own friends, and her own interests in Pennington, and freedom, now, to live her own life.' Harriet smiled as she refilled the coffee cups. 'Mother believes in letting Kitty and me breathe, as she puts it. And expects us to reciprocate.'

'So it was not at her request that decided you to return home to work?'

'No, it was my decision.' She hesitated. 'And it was a convenient move for me at the time.'

'Why, Harriet?'

She told him about Guy Warren, and her realisation that marriage to him would have been a mistake, and Leo's mouth twisted.

'Always it comes back to the question of marriage. And your objections to it.'

Harriet changed the subject swiftly, determined to preserve their fragile truce. 'Now we'd better go up and see how Nonna is before she's settled down for the night.'

Signora Fortinari's face lit up as they entered her room together. She told Claudia to go downstairs for a break. 'She is a good woman,' she confided, when the nurse had bustled out, 'but Harriet's company is far more interesting. I am very fortunate that she was kind enough to come, am I not, Leo?'

'Very fortunate,' he agreed, and took her hand. 'How are you feeling, Nonna?'

'Very much better for seeing you, darling. For seeing both of you,' she added, and smiled radiantly at Harriet. 'Did Silvia give you and Leo a good dinner?' she asked.

So the artful invalid had known all along that Leo would be dining at the villa, thought Harriet, amused. 'Leo tells me you have lots of photograph albums, Nonna. Could I see them sometime?'

The signora was entranced by the idea, and despatched Leo to fetch them. 'Tomorrow,' she told Harriet, 'We shall look at photographs until you beg for mercy.'

When Leo returned with a stack of leather-covered albums, he warned that Nurse Claudia was about to arrive to settle the invalid down for the night. 'So promise me to be good, and rest all you can, Nonna.'

'Of course I will,' she said meekly, and held up her face for Harriet and Leo to kiss her good-night. 'I shall see you tomorrow?' she asked her grandson.

'Without fail,' he assured her.

'I'll be in on my way down to breakfast,' Harriet assured her, and waved from the door as Leo held it open for her.

Downstairs in the hall Leo paused to consult his

watch. 'I must go. I have paperwork to do at home before I go to bed, alas.'

'Thank you for sparing the time to keep me company at dinner,' said Harriet quietly.

'Harriet—' he began, then stopped abruptly, raking his hand through his hair. 'No. It is pointless at this time of night to begin conversations which end in argument. Go to bed, Harriet. You should rest while you can.'

'I'll see you out,' she said, and went outside with him onto the loggia. The evening was cool and crisp, and the stars looked enormous in the dark velvet sky. 'What a beautiful night,' she said, and smiled at him. 'I'm sorry Nonna is ill, but I can't say I'm sorry to be here.'

'I am sorry you are here,' he said harshly.

'But you asked me—'

'I mean,' he said very deliberately, 'that it will make it even harder for me when you go away again.' He took her hand, pressed a kiss into the palm, then ran down to the car, leaving her leaning against a pillar to listen to the sound of his car as it disappeared into the distance.

This, decided Harriet as she went to bed, was silly. Leo wanted her, she loved Leo. What else could possibly matter? Life was too short to deny either herself or Leo happiness, a decision which acted like a sleeping pill, since the next thing she knew it was daylight, and Silvia was tiptoeing in with a cup of tea.

Harriet showered and dried her hair at top speed, pulled on jeans, striped shirt and pullover, and went off to ask about Signora Fortinari's night.

'I slept reasonably well, dear,' said the invalid, holding up her face for Harriet's kiss. 'So did you, I think. You look radiant. Did something happen last night?' she added in a hopeful whisper.

Harriet shook her head, laughing. 'Nothing out of the ordinary. I just slept well, that's all. I'll be back after breakfast to look at those photographs.'

'In an hour, miss,' said the nurse firmly. 'There are things to be done first.'

Harriet wolfed down hot rolls and some fruit, and drank an entire pot of coffee, then jumped up and cleared the table, much to Silvia's disapproval when Harriet took the tray out to the kitchen.

'I must do something to help, Silvia,' she insisted, smiling. 'Isn't it a beautiful day? I'll go for a stroll round the garden until the signora is ready for me.'

When Harriet returned to the sickroom later she found the invalid propped up in a newly-changed bed, wearing a fresh bedjacket and an air of resignation.

'Harriet,' she said with heartfelt relief. 'Now Claudia can go downstairs for well-earned coffee and a long rest while you talk to me.'

When the nurse had gone Harriet grinned as she sat down in her usual chair. 'You look very smart.'

'Smart! I have been given pills, subjected to the indignities of a sponge bath, then propped like a doll in the chair while my bed was changed.' The dark eyes danced wickedly. 'I told Claudia to stay downstairs until lunch unless I called. I think she is offended.'

'You'll bring her round! So what do you feel like now? Shall we go on with the novel, or do you just want to chat?'

'Neither. I would so much like to show you my photographs, dearest. Give me the first album.'

Harriet was fascinated as Vittoria Fortinari turned

page after page which told a pictorial story of her life from just before she was married. The photographs showed a very pretty girl in the bias-cut dresses of the thirties, at parties, and playing tennis and in fancy dress, then in bridal array with a handsome husband, and afterwards with a baby in a christening robe.

'Leo's father, Roberto. There is a picture of Anna, Rosa's mother, in the same robe in a page or two.'

Harriet had seen some of the photographs in silver frames in the salon, but the shots of Leo, Dante and Mirella as children were new to her, and fascinated her most of all. There was Leo playing with his little brother and sister, then as a lordly teenager, with a very young Rosa gazing up at him adoringly, and an older Leo in a formal study with an austerely handsome young woman adorned with a betrothal ring.

'Luisa Bracco?' asked Harriet.

'Yes. She was almost beautiful there, but she has not aged well,' said Nonna with a sniff. 'Though more gracefully than her sister Sophia, who fights advancing years tooth and nail—with the help of Marco Rossi's money.'

Harriet laughed and gave her a hug, then found an album full of parties to celebrate all kinds of occasions.

'I was not Fortinari yet when this one was taken,' Vittoria said sadly, pointing to a shot of two young girls in the long cloaks and oddly eerie masks typical of carnivan Venice. 'That was the last time I saw my cousin.'

'What happened to her?'

'She ran away from home, and died young.' The signora sighed deeply then closed the book. 'No more now. We must not be sad.' Harriet took the albums away and put them on a shelf, then sat down again, lost in thought, as the signora chatted about the happy days her photographs recalled for her. After a while she noticed Harriet's abstraction.

'What is it, darling?'

'Your cousin. What was her name?'

'Chiara. She was so sweet, and I loved her like a sister, but—Harriet, what's the matter?'

Harriet jumped up quickly. 'I'm going to my room to fetch something.' She raced to her room, then returned with a photograph. 'Is *this* your Chiara?'

The signora gazed at the picture in astonishment. Tears welled in her eyes as she looked up at Harriet. 'Dear Lord, that is most certainly my Chiara. A year or so older than when I saw her last, but there's no doubt. How are you in possession of her photograph, Harriet?'

It suddenly struck Harriet that too much emotion was the last thing the signora needed. She sat down by the bed, holding the fragile hand. 'Please don't be upset,' she implored. 'Everyone will be so angry with me if I make you worse.'

'The only thing I'm likely to die of right now,' said Vittoria with asperity, 'is curiosity. So talk, child!'

Harriet obeyed, relating the story of Chiara Russo with as little drama as possible while Vittoria Fortinari listened raptly, hardly able to believe her ears as she found out, at last, what had actually happened to her young cousin. When Harriet had finished, instead of dissolving into tears the invalid smiled joyfully.

'So you are my darling Chiara's granddaughter! No wonder I thought you were my own. Nor that I felt such closeness to your mother the moment we met.

And, of course, this explains your looks. Chiara and I used to be taken for sisters, not cousins, which is why you and Rosa are so much alike. It was Rosa's resemblance to Chiara that always endeared her to me.' She sobered. 'When Chiara ran away her father—he was my mother's brother, and very strict with his only child—would never have her name mentioned again, even after her death. I am so glad to know she found happiness. How grateful I am to Rosa for sending you to me!'

Far from making the invalid worse, the news about Chiara seemed to fill the signora with renewed energy, and she demanded to get up. Only the nurse's threat to call the doctor out kept the rebellious patient in bed.

'Besides, if you get up and have a relapse,' said Harriet, 'everyone will blame me for not looking after you better.'

Which clinched the matter, though nothing could prevent the signora from discussing the amazing revelation all day, especially after Harriet had rung her mother to tell her the news.

Claire was utterly delighted. 'So this makes you some kind of cousin to Leo, then.'

'I suppose it does,' said Harriet, who had thought of that the moment she learned Chiara's connection to the Fortinaris. 'Quite a turn-up.'

'I can't wait to tell Kitty!'

But Harriet was more concerned with Leo's reaction than her sister's. He rang at lunchtime to ask after his grandmother, but Harriet said nothing about the discovery. Nonna had pleaded to be allowed to do that herself, her eyes sparkling at the prospect of telling Leo that Harriet was related to him.

There were several phone calls about the signora's health during the day, including one from Maria Fortinari, who again expressed her thanks to Harriet, and said Mirella was sleeping at that moment, but would love to see Harriet next day if Nonna could spare her.

Harriet felt nervous as she dressed for dinner later. Because the occasion seemed to call for something more formal than trousers and a sweater she put on the pinstriped dress, but left her hair down and hung large amber drops in her ears to offset the frock's severity. When a knock sounded on her door, she threw it open, expecting to see Silvia, or Claudia, then gazed up at Leo in startled surprise.

'*Buona sera.*' He changed to English. 'I am early. I could not wait.'

'You're anxious about Nonna?'

He shook his head, cast a look along the gallery to his grandmother's closed door then pulled Harriet into his arms. 'I cannot go on like this,' he said harshly, leaning his forehead against hers.

'Neither can I,' she whispered. 'But go and see Nonna. She is waiting very impatiently to tell you something.'

Leo stared down at her, a sudden light in his eyes which warned Harriet to step back quickly. 'Later,' she said, smiling incandescently, and he caught her hand in his.

'Come with me to see her,' he said urgently, but she shook her head.

'Nonna wants to talk to you alone.'

'Why?'

'Hurry and you'll find out,' she teased.

It seemed like hours to Harriet before Leo joined

her in the salon. He came in like a whirlwind, shut the door behind him, then swept her into his arms.

'Now we are joined by blood you cannot deny me this!'

Harriet had no intention of denying him anything, a discovery which inflamed Leo to a point where it soon became dangerously obvious that if she didn't call a halt soon she might not be able to. And the thought of Silvia coming in to find them locked together on the floor brought a laugh bubbling up in a way which brought wrath down on her dishevelled head until she let Leo into the joke.

'You are right,' he said ruefully, smoothing her hair. 'You go to my head, *carissima*, and to other parts of me even less easy to control!'

Harriet hugged him, laughing, then she sobered as she looked up into his intent face. 'What is it?'

'We shall discuss it over dinner,' he said firmly, and opened the door for her. 'Then afterwards we shall go up and see Nonna together.'

And to Harriet's frustration Leo refused to explain further until Silvia had provided them with the main course and shut the door behind her.

'I know that marriage does not appeal to you,' began Leo.

'First there's something I should say—' interrupted Harriet, but he held up his hand.

'Let me speak, and then you shall have your say, I promise. It was a great joy to Nonna to discover you were related to her, particularly since the photograph of Chiara Russo cleared up a mystery which had long troubled her.' He smiled at Harriet with a warmth she had never thought to see again. 'It also explained the family resemblance. Though I, for one, always knew you could not be Rosa.'

Harriet raised a disbelieving eyebrow. 'I think you just can't admit being taken in.'

Leo shrugged, laughing at her. 'Certainly not.' He sobered, and laid down his fork. 'Before we go up to Nonna you must know that she very much wants us to marry. She has always wanted that. But now she knows you are Chiara's granddaughter she is utterly determined.'

Harriet pushed her plate away. 'And how do you feel about it?'

'You know how I feel about you,' he said passionately. 'Would it be so hard to pretend for a while that you want to marry me?'

Harriet stared at him blankly. 'Pretend?'

Leo nodded. 'I know that for some reason you dislike the thought of marriage. But Nonna is frail and her heart is not strong, and it would give her so much joy to believe that we would be married one day, an engagement would be a convenient way to satisfy her.'

Harriet stared at him, her mind in a turmoil. She had been fully prepared, up to a few minutes ago, to tell him that she had been so miserable since she last saw him, that she was willing to fall in with his original suggestion.

'By your greeting earlier,' he went on, holding her eyes, 'you obviously had some idea of what Nonna wanted.'

'No, I didn't.' Harriet frowned. 'Could we clarify things a bit?'

He shrugged. 'To me it is crystal clear. I give you a ring, we announce our engagement.' He jumped up, holding out his hand. '*Allora.* Let us go up and make Nonna happy.'

'But Leo,' said Harriet as he rushed her upstairs, 'I haven't said I agree—'

He pulled her into his arms and stifled her protests with a kiss which made nonsense of them. 'Of course you agree, *carissima.* You made that clear earlier, remember.' He knocked on the sickroom door, then drew her inside to smile triumphantly at his expectant grandmother. 'Allow me to introduce my fiancée, Nonna. Will you congratulate me?'

In the end, despite her broad smiles, Nurse Claudia was obliged to put an end to the excitement. 'It is time I settled the signora down for the night,' she said firmly.

Vittoria Fortinari pulled a face, but she complied meekly enough. 'I shall get well very quickly now,' she declared. 'I must get fit for the wedding. Leo, take Harriet out to celebrate. Claudia will look after me.'

In minutes Harriet found herself in the Maserati on the way to Fortino. 'Should we be doing this?' she said anxiously.

'Claudia has the number of my cellphone. We could be back in minutes if we're needed. But in the meantime I'm taking you home.'

'A few words in private are probably a good idea,' said Harriet tartly. 'Nonna mentioned the word wedding. How do we deal with that?'

But Leo refused to discuss it until they were inside the house that Harriet had longed so much to see again. But once they were indoors Leo took her into his arms and began kissing her in a manner which made it all too plain why he'd brought her here.

'This isn't fair,' said Harriet, panting. 'You need to answer some questions.'

'I am doing so,' he said, and smiled at her in a way which caused considerable turbulence under the demure pinstripes. 'I intend to convince you that we belong together.'

'You mean you're going to take me to bed,' said Harriet unevenly.

'Do you object?' He paused abruptly, looking at her with the nearest thing to doubt she'd ever seen in his eyes. 'Harriet, last time I gave you no choice.' He breathed in deeply. 'So this time, even though I want you more than anything I have wanted in my entire life, I shall give you a choice. But if you refuse me, do so quickly, for the love of God!'

Harriet gave him a shaky smile. 'I made my choice long before you brought me here, Leo.'

He closed his eyes for an instant, then seized her in his arms, and she yielded to him wholeheartedly. She wanted Leo Fortinari with such intensity that this time she was as eager as he to reach the room where she had learned her first lesson about the power of love.

'Now we are engaged this is allowed,' he told her hoarsely, and undressed her slowly, his mouth following his hands as they revealed her to him.

'That's sophistry,' she said in English, and Leo laughed and laid her down on the bed.

'It is love, *carissima*,' he corrected. 'I love you, little cousin. Do you love me?'

'I must do,' she said, turning her head away. 'Otherwise—'

'Otherwise you would not be here,' he teased. 'If there is any sophistry involved, my darling, it is

Nonna's. She told me earlier that if I lacked the means to win you round I was no grandson of hers.'

Harriet sat upright in shock. 'You mean this was *Nonna's* idea?'

'No. It was mine. But she approved. And now,' he said, holding her close against him, 'the time for talk is over. I am going to show you how to celebrate this convenient engagement of ours. Ah, Harriet, you are so beautiful, so shy. Look at me.'

Reluctantly she raised her eyes to his, to find them glowing with a look which took her breath away.

'Look at me as we make love,' he commanded softly, 'so that you can see how much I adore you, how much I have longed for you. And this time I promise you will experience the ultimate bliss that man and woman can share *tesoro.*'

Harriet lost herself in his compelling gaze as he caressed her breasts and teased her nipples to quivering life. He slid a slow, relishing hand down her body until it reached the liquid heat which showed how much she wanted him, and she gasped in sudden ecstasy, no longer caring that he witnessed every nuance of her response to the urgent caresses which caused such turbulence inside her. And when she felt she could bear the torment no longer Leo lowered his head, his tongue caressing her to a new pitch of longing, until at last she wanted their union so badly she told him so in sudden, fierce demand, and in triumph he joined his body to hers and began the compelling, breathtaking rhythm that coaxed her, slowly and surely at first, then rapidly and compulsively, along the way to the goal he held her back from relentlessly until he felt her tense and quiver beneath him and at last released his iron control to share in the glory they found together.

Leo held her close in his arms afterwards while their breathing slowed and their thudding hearts resumed a normal rhythm. He raised his head at last and looked down into her wide, astonished eyes.

'What are you thinking?' he whispered.

'It always amazed me that anyone could want to do such an intimate, extraordinary thing.' She smiled up at him. 'If I'd known how it would be I would have done this long ago.'

Leo shook her slightly. 'Do not even think of it. It would not have been the same. You were meant only for me.'

She nodded slowly. 'I know, now, why I never had the slightest desire to make love with anyone else.'

Leo smoothed his hand over her wildly tumbled hair. 'I want so much to think I know the answer to that, but tell me what you mean, *carissima*.'

'It's simple, really.' Harriet smiled up into his intent, possessive face. 'I just couldn't make love with only my body. My heart had to be involved too. Permanently,' she added, just in case he had any doubts.

Leo crushed her to him. 'You admit, at last, that you love me?'

'Yes,' she gasped, and smiled up at him. 'And I'll come to live with you here, if that's what you want.'

He sat up, frowning down at her. 'It is not exactly what I want, Harriet. But I thought it was all you would agree to. Which is why I resorted to blackmail. I thought that if you consented to an engagement I would eventually bring you round to a different view of marriage.'

'I thought it was to please Nonna?' she said unsteadily, suddenly so happy she could hardly breathe.

'It would. But I am not so noble, Harriet. If *I* had not wanted you, not even my beloved grandmother could have persuaded me to such an arrangement.'

'So it's not just convenience?' she demanded.

Leo smiled smugly. 'It will be convenient only if it is the shortest one on record. Is your view of marriage to me different now, my darling?'

'No.'

'*No?*' he said, incensed.

Harriet smiled radiantly. 'It's always been the same. It was you who kept talking about a less formal arrangement.'

Leo pulled her up into his arms. 'You told me you didn't want marriage, little witch.'

'That was when you thought you might have to do the honourable thing and marry me whether you wanted to or not.' She stole a look up at him. 'You're not the only one with pride, Leo Fortinari.'

He kissed her hard, then muttered darkly as the phone rang beside the bed. He barked his name into it, then began to laugh. 'Yes, Nonna.' He listened for a moment. 'Of course I will, Nonna. Sleep well.' He put the phone back, then grinned at Harriet. 'She wants to set a date for the wedding. You *must* marry me now, *tesoro*. Or my pride will never recover.'

They collapsed together, laughing, then Leo pulled up the covers and held Harriet close. 'Just a few minutes more like this, my darling, then I must take you back to the villa. Nonna told me not to keep you out all night.'

'So she was pleased?' said Harriet, wriggling closer.

'Almost as much as I am,' he said huskily. 'We shall go to Arezzo to buy a ring tomorrow,' he promised, and kissed her. 'I was clever, no?'

'In what way?'

'I knew that once I had my ring on your finger I would never let you go.'

'The thought *had* occurred to me, too,' she said demurely, and he laughed in delight and began to kiss and caress her in a way which meant it was hours, rather than minutes before Leo Fortinari reluctantly parted with his cousin several times removed on the loggia of the Villa Castiglione.

'Tell me again that you love me,' he demanded as he kissed Harriet good-night, then looked up with a frown as Nurse Claudia appeared, with obvious embarrassment, to interrupt them.

'The signora will not settle until she has seen you, Signor Leo. And it is very late. I shall make her a hot drink while you say good-night.'

Harriet exchanged a grin with Leo as they hurried upstairs to share their happiness with Vittoria Fortinari.

'I have already informed your mother, Leo,' said the radiant invalid. 'But in the morning you must ring your mother, Harriet, also Rosa in Paris.'

'And you must rest,' said Leo firmly. 'Here comes Claudia to show us out.'

When happy good-nights had been said Leo put an arm round Harriet as they went downstairs. 'It is late and I must go,' he sighed, as they went outside on the loggia.

Harriet leaned against him, frowning thoughtfully as she gazed up at the stars. 'I'll give notice to

Roedale, but I might have to work until they find a replacement.'

Leo groaned in despair. 'I had forgotten that.'

'I'm used to having a job,' she reminded him warily. 'I don't have to teach, but I'd like to do work of some kind after we're married.'

He held her close. 'With your fluency in languages you could be of much help to me on the marketing side at Fortino. Would you like that, *carissima?*'

'You bet I would,' she assured him joyfully.

They were silent for a while, reluctant to part, and for the time being content just to be in each other's arms.

'I must ring Kitty in the morning, too,' said Harriet after a while. 'And my boss at the firm, and Dr Rushworth, the Head at Roedale—'

'And I must ring my father and Dante in California, also Tony and Allegra.' Leo shook his head. 'I can see I should have married Luisa Bracco after all, if only to avoid astronomic telephone bills!'

'And acquire her vineyards at the same time,' Harriet said tartly.

Leo said something very rude and idiomatic in Italian about Luisa's vineyards, then turned Harriet's face up to his and looked deep into her eyes. 'I have all I want in life here in my arms,' he said, in his husky, accented English which evoked such a storm of response from Harriet it was a long time before Leo let her go.

She smiled up at him, then locked her arms round his spare waist and laid her head on his chest, against the heart she could feel thudding against her cheek. 'My sentiments exactly,' said Harriet, then said it again in Italian to press home her point.

HARLEQUIN ◆ PRESENTS®

Passion™

Looking for stories that **sizzle?**

Wanting a read that has
a little extra **spice?**

Harlequin Presents® is thrilled to bring
you romances that turn up the **heat!**

In November 1999 there's *The Revenge Affair*
by Susan Napier, Harlequin Presents® #2062

Every other month there'll be a
PRESENTS PASSION book by one of your
favorite authors.

And in January 2000 look out for
One Night with his Wife by Lynne Graham,
Harlequin Presents® #2073

*Pick up a **PRESENTS PASSION**—
where **seduction** is guaranteed!*

Available wherever Harlequin books are sold.

HARLEQUIN®
Makes any time special ™

Visit us at www.romance.net   HPPAS5

Looking For More Romance?

Visit Romance.net

Look us up on-line at: http://www.romance.net

Check in daily for these and other exciting features:

Hot off the press

View all current titles, and purchase them on-line.

What do the stars have in store for you?

Horoscope

Hot deals

Exclusive offers available only at Romance.net

Plus, don't miss our interactive quizzes, contests and bonus gifts.

PWEB

HARLEQUIN PRESENTS®

Seduction
SWEET REVENGE

They wanted to get even.
Instead they got...married!

by bestselling author

Penny Jordan

Don't miss Penny Jordan's latest enthralling miniseries
about four special women. Kelly, Anna, Beth and Dee
share a bond of friendship and a burning desire to
avenge a wrong. But in their quest for revenge, they
each discover an even stronger emotion.
Love.

Look out for all four books in Harlequin Presents®:

November 1999
THE MISTRESS ASSIGNMENT

December 1999
LOVER BY DECEPTION

January 2000
A TREACHEROUS SEDUCTION

February 2000
THE MARRIAGE RESOLUTION

Available at your favorite retail outlet.

HARLEQUIN®
Makes any time special ™

Look us up on-line at: http://www.romance.net   HPSRS

"This book is DYNAMITE!"
—Kristine Rolofson

"A riveting page turner…"
—Joan Elliott Pickart

"Enough twists and turns to keep everyone
guessing… What a ride!"
—Jule McBride

See what all your favorite authors
are talking about.

Coming October 1999 to a retail store near you.

Look us up on-line at: http://www.romance.net   PHQ4993

In celebration of Harlequin®'s golden anniversary

Enter to win a *dream!* You could win:

- A luxurious trip for two to *The Renaissance Cottonwoods Resort* in Scottsdale, Arizona, or

- A bouquet of flowers once a week for a year from **FTD**, or

- A $500 shopping spree, or

- A fabulous bath & body gift basket, including **K-tel**'s *Candlelight and Romance* 5-CD set.

Look for **WIN A DREAM** flash on specially marked Harlequin® titles by Penny Jordan, Dallas Schulze, Anne Stuart and Kristine Rolofson in October 1999*.

*No purchase necessary—for contest details send a self-addressed envelope to Harlequin Makes Any Time Special Contest, P.O. Box 9069, Buffalo, NY, 14269-9069 (include contest name on self-addressed envelope). Contest ends December 31, 1999. Open to U.S. and Canadian residents who are 18 or over. Void where prohibited.

PHMATS-GR

Coming Next Month

HARLEQUIN PRESENTS®

THE BEST HAS JUST GOTTEN BETTER!

#2061 THE MISTRESS ASSIGNMENT Penny Jordan
(Sweet Revenge/Seduction)
Kelly has agreed to act the seductress in order to teach a lesson to the man who betrayed her best friend. It's a scheme fraught with danger—especially when gorgeous stranger Brough Frobisher gets caught in the cross fire....

#2062 THE REVENGE AFFAIR Susan Napier
(Presents Passion)
Joshua Wade was convinced that Regan was plotting to disrupt their wedding. Regan had to admit there was unfinished business between them—a reckless one-night stand.... She had good reason for getting close to Joshua, though, but she could never reveal her secret plans....

#2063 SLADE BARON'S BRIDE Sandra Marton
(The Barons)
When Lara Stevens and Slade Baron were both facing an overnight delay in an airport, Slade suggested they spend the time together. Who would she hurt if Lara accepted his invitation? He wanted her, and she wanted . . . his child!

#2064 THE BOSS'S BABY Miranda Lee
(Expecting!)
When Olivia's fiancé ditched her, her world had been blown apart and with it, her natural caution. She'd gone to the office party and seduced her handsome boss! But now Olivia has a secret she dare not tell him!

#2065 THE SECRET DAUGHTER Catherine Spencer
Soon after Joe Donnelly's sizzling night with Imogen Palmer, she'd fled. Now ten years on, Joe was about to uncover an astonishing story—one that would culminate in a heartrending reunion with the daughter he never knew he had.

#2066 THE SOCIETY GROOM Mary Lyons
(Society Weddings)
When Olivia meets her former lover, rich socialite Dominic FitzCharles, at a society wedding, he has a surprise for her: he announces their betrothal to the press, in front of London's elite. Just how is Olivia supposed to say no?